SEAN SHEEHAN

Maze

Short Stories to Faze

This edition first published in paperback by
Michael Terence Publishing in 2022
www.mtp.agency

ISBN 9781800943797

Michael Terence
Publishing

Contents

The Maze

Clever how it connects

On entering the maze, the boy suddenly became aware of a ringing mobile phone. The phone was ringing in the distance from somewhere within the maze. He was drawn to the ringing phone; it became an irresistible force drawing him forward. He turned left, he turned right drawn by the sound of the phone. He was getting closer and closer to the sound of the ringing phone.

***

'I'm sorry dear, it got lost in the maze,' the old man remarked to Mary. The old man, Mr Donovan, was in Talbot's supermarket looking for some jam; he had requested help from Mary, the shop assistant. He was accompanied by his wife Maeve, who was pushing the trolley. 'Sometimes a thought pops into my head and then gets lost in the maze in my head. I just forgot the aisle where the jam was.'

Mary helped him find the section of the supermarket where the jam was located. Mary was familiar with the old couple as they were regulars at Talbot's supermarket. Always smiling, they sometimes held hands, their love for each other clear for the world to see. Mr Donovan always pushed the trolley and always carried the bags. Mr Donovan was sprightlier and moved with greater ease than his wife. When they were about to leave the supermarket, they always paused and checked with each other that they had not forgotten anything.

On their way out Mr Donovan broke away from his wife and spoke to Mary.

'Sure we've been married for fifty years but she's still got the sweetest smile in the world. In her younger days she was a singer. When she sings an Irish ballad, she breaks your heart. Good luck,' and he waved Mary and Daphne goodbye.

Mary and her friend Daphne, who were working on the self-service tills, often said to each other that a large slice of human life was here at Talbot's. This went some way to satisfying their boundless curiosity. They watched the old couple leave the supermarket.

'That might be me one day with my future husband.'

Long-time friends Daphne proclaimed her individuality by her Goth appearance; Mary proclaimed her individuality by her refusal to wear make-up. Mary was small and plump whereas Daphne was tall with broad shoulders. On the same wavelength strange ideas and weird observations bounced off them as naturally as night followed day.

***

Talbot's supermarket was characterised by high ceilings and many signs dotted at regular intervals, battering the human brain with information. Like any other supermarket Talbot's retail space was based around division and precision. Row upon row of shelves containing food and goods for sale, allocated their own space and numbered with exact information about what was for sale. Each section was precisely labelled.

At that moment one of their colleagues, Henry, bounded up to Mary. Tall and thin he was bookish; some people described him as a nerd. He liked to spring questions upon them. He looked at Mary.

'Are you a somnambulist?'

'What's that when it's at home?' replied Mary defeated. Daphne looked perplexed.

'Sleepwalking!' Henry replied victorious.

'No, I'm not,' Mary said clearly irritated.

'Well one of our customers might be a somnambulist… look behind you!'

Mary and Daphne looked behind them and saw a young woman, wearing a pair of pyjamas, in the queue for one of the staffed tills. Mary and Daphne looked at each other bemused.

***

Each week Albert shopped at Talbot's supermarket to purchase cat food for his cat Misty. Behind the melancholy face there was a devoted cat lover. Mary and Daphne had Albert pegged as creepy man on account of his prolonged stare when he talked to you. Mary had just returned from her break, when walking through the cat food section she suddenly came across creepy man staring at the shelves. He looked around and noted the presence of a member of staff.

'Excuse me I'm looking for kibbles the cat food?'

'I'm afraid we're out of stock at the moment. We're waiting for a delivery. What about cat nuggets?' she said pointing to the top shelf. 'They come in different meat varieties, chicken, beef.'

'Sounds great. Misty likes beef,' he said stretching his hand to the top shelf to pick up a packet. 'You know my neighbour, a vegetarian social worker, tried to feed his cat a vegetarian diet.'

Albert's stare was now trained on Mary.

'Not a good idea!'

'Exactly. Cats are carnivores. Like me.' He paused. 'Are you a carnivore or a vegetarian?'

Mary was disturbed by his intense stare and was thrown completely by his weird question. The question hung in the air unanswered. She smiled, remained silent and took her leave. Creepy man lived up to his reputation.

***

The little boys' balloon had escaped from his hand and began to ascend above the garden. The boy watched it rise above his house. He went through the kitchen, past the living room where his mother was ironing some clothes. He opened the front door and followed the balloon in the sky, along the pavement.

Albert was walking down the same street at the time on the other side of the road. He saw the boy looking upward toward the sky. He stared at the boy. He was now locked in a trance, a predatory trance. He decided to cross the road. Meanwhile the boys' mother realised that he was not in the house and she darted to the front door and emerged on the street. Albert saw a woman further down the road, shouting the name Terry. The boy stopped and looked back at the woman. Albert stopped himself from crossing the road, unlocking himself from his trance. The boy began to walk toward the woman, and they walked back to the house from which they had emerged.

***

After work Albert sometimes visited the maze in the local park. He was fascinated by the maze, its endless, silent paths. He regularly walked around the maze; he found that it cleared his head. He had walked around the maze so many times that he knew every inch of the maze. He knew the times of day it was busy and when it was not busy. He used to watch boys and girls walking around the park and in and out of the maze. One day walking around the maze he conceived a plan, a plan that could only be described as demonic. He recalled that he had a bottle of chloroform at home, a bottle that he had stolen whilst working in a pharmacy. The possession of chloroform was central to his plan. Albert kept on thinking of the plan, turning it over and over in his head. Would he have the will to execute his plan? It turned out that Albert did have the will to execute his plan.

***

Albert lived alone in his council house with his cat Misty. The house was sparsely furnished and decorated with dark colours. There were no family photographs. Albert had no friends. Every evening Albert logged into his computer. He had a fascination with and dexterity at information technology that had developed alongside his job selling mobile phones. Albert was viewed by his colleagues at work as an oddball. His colleagues had no idea that nearly every evening he surfed the dark web. Albert usually visited the same illegal websites.

Albert gave Misty her tea; she ate her kibbles with relish, to Albert's delight. He made himself a cup of coffee with two sugars (Albert had a sweet tooth). He then sat down in front of his laptop for his evening recreation. Misty had finished her tea and was now curled up on the settee. Albert stared at Misty and then opened his laptop. He went straight to his favourite illegal website and in so doing left human civilisation behind. Albert's brain was excited and thrilled by the thousands of images he viewed. These images may be vile, cruel and depraved but Albert had an insatiable hunger for them.

The doorbell rang. Albert woke up from his reverie. Albert's pizza delivery had arrived pulling him away from his computer screen.

***

Mr and Mrs Donovan lived in a small council house in the local area. Staunch Catholics they attended church every Sunday, said their prayers every day and whenever they passed the Catholic church on the high street they both acknowledged it silently, giving the sign of the cross. Mrs Donovan was sitting at home, sewing a button into her husbands' shirt. She had done this task many times before, her dexterity in this quite apparent. Her husband sat in an adjacent armchair quietly watching the BBC news. After fifty years of marriage, they knew each other's habits and quirks.

'I don't know if it's my age or what, but the roads around here seem to get more confusing,' said Mr Donovan. 'The other day I got lost.'

'Ah sure, you're not twenty-four anymore,' Mrs Donovan said quietly.

At that moment the phone rang. Mrs Donovan answered it. It was her friend from the line dancing group she attended. Her friend was inquiring as to why she had not attended the group on Tuesday and to make sure that she was ok.

'You know May it totally went out of my head. I'll see you next week,' Mrs Donovan declared. She put down the phone and turned to her husband. 'I forgot about the line dancing group last week,' she said smiling gently.

'Ah sure you're getting on,' he replied with a smile on his face. 'I meant to say to you that I found a song sheet on top of the wardrobe in the bedroom last week.'

'A song sheet?' she said looking perplexed.

'Yes. She Moved Through the Fair. 'He got up and moved to the nearby cabinet, opened a drawer and removed a sheet of paper and handed it to his wife. 'Maeve you have the voice of an angel. Remember that time you sang that song in the pub in Tipperary? That was a beautiful rendition.'

Mrs Donovan looked at the song sheet, her eyes moistened, and she smiled gently.

'Thank you Ted, I loved singing that song.'

Set in rural Ireland She Moved Through the Fair is a folk song about thwarted love. A man watches the woman he loves move through a fair and she tells him that since her family will approve the wedding it will not be long before our wedding day. But he never sees her again. Later the man dreams that she visits him; again, she tells him,' It will not be long til our wedding day. In another version of the story the woman is a ghost. But the wedding does not happen; the reason for this is obscure.'

***

When Pat received the news that his brother had died in Ireland, he made immediate arrangements to travel there for the funeral. Funerals in rural Ireland were organised quickly. His wife Maeve, who knew his brother well, would accompany him. His brother, Seamus, had died of a heart attack at the age of eighty.

Going back to Ireland would be an emotional journey, made

more so by the fact that it was for a funeral. They hired a car from Dublin airport and drove to Mountrath, county Laoise. Maeve drove the car. Pat noted the Gaelic Road signs. These were beloved images of his childhood, small rectangular pieces of metal on a pole, with a white background and dark lettering. The outward edge of the sign assumed the shape of an arrow. The Gaelic signs told Pat and Maeve that it was over hundred miles to Mountrath from Dublin.

As they drove through Dublin, they noted that Dublin was now full of glittering, shiny pieces of architecture. It was a brave new world that filled Pat with dismay. The Ireland that Pat grew up in was a distant memory.

As they approached Laoise Pat noted the proliferation of roundabouts. These images pushed aside his memory of the old, grey Irish country roads.

'What's that? A community alert area? inquired Pat.

He noticed the sign as they approached Mountrath.

'That's the new system for reporting crime and suspicious types and vehicles in the area,' said Maeve.

'Well that's a sign of the times. They didn't have those in my day!' he retorted.

'You're surely right their Pat!'

When they arrived at Trumera Pat recognised it immediately. He remembered the curves in the country road and each house on the way to his brothers' house even though the light was fading. A huge arc light was positioned outside the house of his brother, trailing cables to the house, providing light on the dark country road. People milled outside the house, making their way to the front of the house. Several cars were parked outside the house. Pat saw the elderly woman approach the car. He had no idea who she was. Maeve saw the confusion on her husband's face.

'It's Sarah. Seamus's wife.'

'Oh!'

When they got out of the car Sarah flung her arms around Pat and then embraced Maeve. They looked at each other and cried. The house was saturated with people paying their respects. Neighbours, cousins moved from room to room. The kichen and dining room were replete with food, cold meats, sandwiches and soft drinks, in keeping with a traditional Irish wake.

Seamus' body and coffin were in the back room. The room was deathly silent, several people lining the walls, quiet and solemn. They would break the silence to greet people as they entered the room. Pat had already told Maeve that he did not want to see his brothers' body.

Pat and Maeve went into the living room and sat on a sofa. People were huddled together, talking and reminiscing. The wall was lined with pictures of the Virgin Mary and Jesus Christ.

'He was a great farmer,' said burly Mick a neighbour.

'He liked a joke,' said Helen a shop assistant in the local grocery store.

'He had a wicked sense of humour!' reiterated Mick.

And they all laughed, including Maeve and Pat. Then the room went quiet. Sarah, red-eyed and emotional, looked at Maeve. People in the room drank their tea.

'Seamus loved your singing Maeve. Will you sing us a song?'

'Ah do,' implored Peter a first cousin of Seamus.

Maeve gave a gentle smile. The room went silent. Pat rubbed her knee and grasped her hand. Maeve readied herself and then began to sing. She looked upward.

'My young love said to me

My mother wasn't mind

And my father won't slight you

For your lack of kind

Then she stepped away from me

And this she did say

It will not be long love
Till our wedding day
She stepped away from me
And she moved through the fair
And fondly I watched her
Moved here and moved there
Then she made her way homeward
With one star awake
As the swan in the evening
Moves over the lake.'

The room was hushed throughout. Pat was always choked up with emotion after listening to Maeve sing this song.

After the funeral Pat motioned his wife to come with him. They walked up the country lane, for about a mile and then turned left. They followed the curve in the road until they came to a small bridge. The boundary of the road was marked by a stone wall. They stopped and looked over the side of the bridge. Below was a railway line.

'That's the railway line. The train comes from Portlaiose and then heads for Dublin and Belfast. As a boy I used to sit here and wait for the train. When it passed underneath I'd wave at the train and the train driver would wave back.'

Maeve grasped Pat's hand. Pat and Maeve had no idea that the body of a fourteen-year-old boy had been discovered in woodland near their home. And that the police wanted to interview Pat as part of their ongoing inquiries.

***

When they returned to London Pat and Maeve were shocked to discover that not only had there been a murder near their home, but the victim was a fourteen-year-old boy.

Maeve was watching the television whilst Pat was absorbed in the newspaper. A smile appeared on Maeve's face as soon as she heard the Irish melodies of the Nolans singing the song I'm In the Mood for Dancing.

'Are sure aren't they lovely. Lovely girls with lovely voices,' she declared.

'From county Clare I believe,' said Pat lifting his head up from the newspaper.

'No Pat they are from Dublin. Didn't their da sing in the ballrooms of Dublin. Then the daughters got involved. They moved to Blackpool…'

'And the rest is history,' said Pat.

Still absorbed in his newspaper Pat was studying an article called the hidden object. The cartoon contained a sea of ice creams, each one with expressive faces. The object of the exercise was to find the lollipop amongst the sea of ice creams.

'Look at this Maeve. The cartoon contains a hidden object. A lollipop. Sure, I can't see it!'

Maeve stood up from her armchair and moved to her husband, bending over to study the newspaper. She studied the cartoon carefully. Suddenly she let out an exclamation.

'There! In the left-hand corner. There's the lollipop!'

She pointed to an area of the cartoon. Pat looked and saw the lollipop.

'Maeve… you're a wonder so's you are.'

***

The police were conducting door to door enquiries following the murder of the boy. Maeve answered the door to a small, well-dressed man who introduced himself as detective Peter Sugden. Courteous and giving off a strong scent of after-shave Maeve invited him into the front room. Pat introduced himself to the detective and after sitting down on the sofa he began asking questions.

'Were either of you in the woods or near the woods near Lincoln Park on Monday sixth of August?'

'No. I was at home watching the television,' said Maeve.

'I was out in the park for my daily walk,' said Pat.

'What time was that?'

'I usually go midday just after my lunch at about twelve thirty.'

'The Park is adjacent to the woods where the boy was found. Can you remember who you saw that day,' probed the detective.

'Well my memory is not great these days. I think I saw a young woman pushing a pram. There wasn't many people in the park that day as far as I can remember.'

'Did you see a boy, small with dark hair wearing a school uniform?'

'No I did not see a boy. I visited the maze that day.'

'The maze in the park?'

'Yes, I remember I walked around the maze.'

'Did you see anybody acting suspiciously… hanging around?'

'No.'

'OK. Well thanks for your time. If you remember anything no matter how insignificant give me a ring. Here's my card.'

The detective handed his card to Pat.

'I will so.'

At that the detective stood up and took his leave.

***

One of Pat's pastimes, whilst he was out for his daily walk, was to stop and watch work at various construction sites around London. Pat noted roadworks occurring on a nearby road, a main artery of the London transport network. Pat would stand, hands behind his back, and watch workers dig up the road with loud machinery. Occasionally he would strike up a conversation with a worker. During his working years he was a carpenter and joiner by trade. Yesterday he noted that the local railway station had scaffolding erected for the purpose of maintenance work.

***

Every week Pat and Maeve went to the Café in the shopping mall to have afternoon tea. Both had scones, clotted cream and raspberry jam. The waitress knew them by name. It was a simple, quiet ritual.

That Tuesday the mall was thronged with people of every age. As the retail expert would say footfall was high. As Pat sipped her cup of tea, she noticed a familiar figure walking around the shopping mall. She leaned forward looking at Pat intently.

'It's your man, the long fella,' she said.

'Albert,' said Pat looking around.

Albert was a middle-aged man who lived next door to them. They referred to him as the long fella because of his physical resemblance to the first president of the Irish Republic, Eamon De Valera. He was tall and had a thin, long face.

'I'm not sure he belongs to the human race Pat,' said Maeve.

'He'd never give you the time of the day… but he loves his cat. It takes all sorts to make up the world!' asserted Pat.

Afterward they strolled around the mall looking in shopping windows. Maeve went to use the public toilet and asked Pat to buy a newspaper from WH Smith. Pat looked around, walking for a couple of minutes and suddenly realised he could not remember where the WH Smith was located. The shopping mall became a vast mystery, a mix of strange sounds and images, a collection of unfamiliar shops. He found his way back to the concourse area near the public toilets and found his wife waiting for him.

'Sorry Maeve, the Daily Mail was sold out.'

Pat never lied to his wife but this time he felt he had no choice, to save himself from the embarrassment of admitting that he could not find the shop.

***

One morning Pat decided to remove some old cans of paint from his shed. Unbeknownst to Pat whilst doing this his neighbours' cat Misty had crept into the shed and hid behind a box. When he completed his task, he closed the shed thereby trapping Misty in the shed.

Pat and Maeve were surprised one evening when their mysterious, aloof neighbour knocked on the door. Maeve answered the door to be faced with the reincarnation of Eamon DeValera. To Maeve's surprise his stony face transformed into a smile.

'Hi. I think my cat Misty is trapped in your shed.'

'Your cat is in our shed! Well, come in. Let's have a look, come in' said a concerned Maeve.

Albert followed Maeve through the house until they came to the garden. Pat joined them in the garden.

'Albert thinks his cat is trapped in our shed,' she said addressing her husband.

Maeve went to the shed and opened the shed door. There, lo and behold, was Misty sitting on a rung of a ladder.

'My God you're right,' said Maeve.

Albert went into the shed and picked up the cat.

'Sure I was in the shed this morning clearing out some old paint cans. He must have sneaked in there when I wasn't looking,' declared Pat.

At that moment Pat's mobile phone rang. He spoke brusquely into the phone telling the caller he did not need life insurance and then ending the call.

'You've got an older model of a Nokia phone,' declared Albert whose attention was captured by the device.

'That's right,' said Pat.

'You should get a smartphone like this,' whereupon Albert produced a phone from his pocket. 'I work for a mobile phone company. That ringtone you've got is the Nokia tune. The best ringtone is the Marimba ringtone. Here ring my number 0778886683.'

Pat humoured Albert as he seemed so animated about the subject, and he rang the number. Albert's number rang, emitting the distinctive ringtone, soulless and repetitive.

'Isn't that a great ringtone. I'd get rid of that phone if I were you. Anyhow at least Misty is safe and well.'

Misty was getting impatient on Albert's arm and clearly wanted to go.

'Well I'm very sorry about that,' said an embarrassed Pat.

At that Albert took his leave.

***

In the darkness of the confession box Pat gathered his thoughts. Gathering his thoughts these days was more difficult than usual. Through the grill he saw the outline of a head, that would be Father McCarthy.

Pat confessed that he had been drinking heavily and that he used the concealment provided by the maze in his local park to consume his bottle of whiskey. Also, to his eternal regret he once swore at his beloved wife Maeve. If there was an angel on God's earth, then Maeve was that angel he told Father McCarthy.

Father McCarthy instructed him to say three Hail Marys' and four Our Fathers.' Then Pat took his exit from the confession box. As he walked away from the confession box, he heard a ringing mobile phone. He had inadvertently left his mobile phone in the confession box. He opened the door of the confession box and saw the bright light in the looming darkness and picked up the phone. When he answered his phone there was silence on the other end.

***

It was a bright summers day, a Tuesday, when something extraordinary happened to Pat. He and Maeve were walking home after he picked up Maeve from her lining dancing class. Watching her dance, in slow rhythmic moves to the sound of Irish music, lifted his heart.

A busy road, they always used the zebra crossing to cross the road. Maeve pressed the button, to activate the traffic lights. The beeping noise and the green light on the black box indicated that it was safe to cross the road. Maeve and Pat advanced toward the zebra crossing. But suddenly Pat froze. Looking down at the zebra crossing he saw a hole.

'Come on Pat… the lights will change if we don't hurry!' implored Maeve.

'I can't,' said Pat emphatically.

Maeve saw the look of terror on his face and was totally baffled.

'Alright Pat. We won't cross here. We'll cross further on up the road,' she reassured Pat.

They walked back to the pavement and continued walking on up the road. They crossed the road without incident. They were both silent. Maeve asked herself: what just happened?

***

Maeve and Pat had, for some time, entered a silent pact, not to talk about changes in Pat's behaviour. But the incident at the zebra crossing had caused her alarm. Taken all together, the memory lapses, not recognising his sister-in-law at his brothers' wake, prompted Maeve to talk to her husband and report her concerns to a doctor.

The doctor told Pat and Maeve that he would need to undergo a brain scan and a cognitive test. Pat readily agreed to these tests. Maeve squeezed his hand for moral support as the doctors' consultation concluded.

***

Sitting at The Café in the shopping mall Pat and Maeve enjoyed their cream scone, raspberry jam and cup of tea, a ritual they never grew tired of. The shopping mall was quite busy.

'Lovely scones Pat.'

'Lovely scones Maeve.'

'It's Dana's birthday today, she's sixty-eight according to the newspaper.'

'Sure all Kinds of Everything is a beautiful song. The Eurovision song contest was never the same after she won it. And I believe she's a kithogue like yourself.'

'All the best singers are left-handed, so I'm in good company. Was Jim Reeves a kithogue I wonder?'

'I don't know Maeve.'

Maeve and Pat had both purchased a new mobile phone. In the parlance of the day, they had upgraded. She put down her scone and removed her new phone from her handbag. She studied it intently. She was fascinated by the touch screen facility on the smartphone.

'You can forget about buttons and keyboards on your old phone now Pat. Now it's touch screen.'

'What's an app Maeve?'

'Well Pat I read an article about it in the paper. An app is a computer thing that you can install on your smartphone. So, you can install a McDonald's app on your phone and order a takeaway!'

'Maeve I think the software in my brain is turning to mush!'

'And young couples send each other emojis.'

'Sure what's an emoji?

'Well it's a little round thing in a text message and when a fella wants to tell his girlfriend he loves her he sends her a heart shaped emoji!'

At the next table a young couple were chatting when the young man's mobile phone started to ring. Pat instantly recognised the ringtone on the mobile phone. It was the same ringtone Albert advised him to get. He remembered sitting on the bench in the maze in the park, on the day before the boy was found dead. He remembered hearing the ringing mobile phone in the near distance of the maze. The same ringtone on Albert's mobile phone.

At that moment he knew that Albert was involved in the murder of the boy. He did see Albert in the park that day. Maeve noted the change in his facial expression.

'What's the matter Pat?'

'I need to talk to detective Collins.'

***

Pat decided to contact detective Collins. The detective visited Pat at home. Maeve greeted him at the door and brought him into the living room where Pat was waiting for him. He sat down on the sofa.

'You wanted to talk to me?'

'Yes. That day, that Monday I remembered a few more things.'

'Good.'

'I saw my neighbour, Albert in the park that day. Albert… The long fella that's what Meave calls him. He sells mobile phones. He was walking near the maze.'

'The maze?'

'I go there sometimes.' Here he stopped to check that his wife was in the kitchen, out of earshot. 'I sit in the bench in the middle of the maze and have a quiet drink of whiskey, for privacy like…'

'Sure. 'Detective Collins nodded; he understood completely.

'Well whilst I was having a nice drink, I heard the mobile phone ringing. It kept on ringing for about four or five minutes…'

'You heard a mobile phone ringing from inside the maze?'

'Definitely… then I heard a muffled sound…'

'A muffled sound like somebody trying to talk, but being stopped from talking?'

'Yes. Then the mobile phone stopped ringing.'

'Did you see Albert in the maze?'

'No.'

'Thanks Pat. You've been very helpful.'

At that detective Collins took his leave.

***

The Paterson maze was named after the local businessman Paul Paterson. He grew wealthy after establishing a factory that produced car batteries. He established a fund that financed the ongoing maintenance and upkeep of the maze.

The Paterson maze was rectangular in shape. With its symmetrical unity, straight lines and exactness a maze is a thing of beauty that gives endless pleasure to the eye. A thing of mystery. A puzzle. You got lost in a maze and children loved the challenge of finding the exit.

For Pat it provided a secret place where he could drink without being seen or judged. The second time he visited the maze Pat helped a boy find his football after he had accidentally kicked his football in the maze. He also helped the boy find his way out of the maze. But now he wondered: was the maze the scene of a crime?

***

The autopsy of the boy revealed that he died of strangulation. He had been sexually assaulted. The coroner informed detective Collins that there were traces of chloroform around his mouth. His attacker had rendered him unconscious by chloroform. The detective brought Albert to the station for questioning and obtained a court order to seize his mobile phone and laptop.

The laptop revealed child pornography. But the police technical assistant who examined the two mobile phones discovered a crucial piece of information: that both phones were active in the area near the woods on the day before the human remains of the boy were found.

The police search of his house did not find any chloroform. But looking into Albert's background the detective discovered that he once had worked in a pharmacy.

***

When Pat and Maeve returned from the doctors' appointment they were quiet and subdued. Maeve went to the kitchen and put the kettle on.

'Sit down Pat, I'll make us a nice cup of tea.'

Pat removed his coat, turned on the television and sat down on the sofa. The diagnosis was clear. After various scans and tests he was diagnosed with Alzheimer's disease. The incident on the zebra crossing was a symptom of the condition, causing a distortion in spatial awareness.

Maeve brought in a cup of tea for Pat and a cup of tea for herself. The news was on the television.

'Well you can start the tablets today,' said Maeve.

'I will sure,' said Pat.

'I'll make us a nice stew for tea,' said Maeve.

***

Detective Collins ordered a group of police officers to search the maze. Meanwhile he walked around the maze, noting the sizable area it encompassed and the location of the entrance and the exit. The exit was located near the woodland where the remains of the murder victim was found. He walked around the maze himself, noting the hedges were over six foot. He stopped and tried to imagine the chain of events that led up to the murder.

Suddenly a police officer shouted that he found something. Detective Collins was near the centre of the maze and rushed to the officer. The officer held a handerkerchief in his hand. It had a particular aroma. Detective Collins put on his gloves and smelt the handkerchief.

'Chloroform!' he exclaimed.

The handkerchief was located near the centre of the maze where the bench was positioned. The detective now had a clear idea of what happened to the unfortunate victim.

***

The interview room at the police station consisted of a table and four chairs. Detective Collins sat on one side of the table, a sheet of foolscap paper in front of him. A pen lay alongside the paper. Albert sat on chair looking relaxed and unperturbed. His composure bordered on arrogance given the gravity of the offence he was being questioned about. Sitting next to him was his legal representative, a sharply dressed woman in her twenties, looking solemn and pensive.

There was a black box on the edge of the table that recorded the interview. Detective Collins pressed a button on the box and stated the date and time the interview commenced, and the people present at the interview. The atmosphere was tense.

'You know why we're here Albert?' Albert nodded his head. 'We're here to investigate the murder of Allen Turpin, a fourteen-year-old schoolboy. So, were you in Paterson Park on the seventh

August this year?'

'Yes, I was. I was having my daily walk. 'he said calmly.

'Did you see Allen Turpin?'

'No,' Albert asserted.

'The Paterson maze, do you like walking around the Paterson maze?'

'I walk around it sometimes,' again Albert was totally unperturbed.

'Mazes, they are fascinating things aren't they Albert? All those paths weaving in and out. Intersections, dead ends and U bends they are really fascinating,' Detective Collins said pressing the point.

'They are ok,' Albert said looking uninterested.

'I think Albert you know that maze like the back of your hand. It was all part of your plan. You know how to get in and get out of the maze quickly. You studied the maze. You knew at that time of day the maze was quiet, with hardly any visitors. You saw Allen walking around the park. So, then you decided to initiate your plan. You sell mobile phones don't you Albert?'

'That's right I sell mobile phones. Perfectly lawful.'

'You know all about ringtones. So, you entered the maze and positioned one of your mobiles on the floor of a U bend near the centre of the maze. I think you do that regularly; on the off chance that a potential victim enters the maze. You own two mobile phones. You turned this mobile phone on and set the ringtone to its maximum volume so the ringing would carry. You quickly exited the maze and saw the boy wandering around the park. You watched him from a distance. Then bingo you saw him approach the maze. You saw him enter the maze via the entrance. You ran to the exit. Once you reached the exit you rang your second mobile phone sitting on the floor of the maze. You made your way into the maze, moving rapidly, heartbeat racing to the location of the second mobile phone. Allen, on hearing the mobile phone would be drawn by its incessant ringing. When Allen arrived at the source of the ringing, he saw the phone on the floor of the maze. On a U bend of the maze. You were on the other side of the U bend with a chloroformed handkerchief at the ready. You overpowered him and the chloroform rendered him unconscious. You then took him to the nearby woods, sexually assaulted Allen Turpin and murdered him.'

'You can't prove anything,' Albert said with a sneer.

'We've got DNA evidence. Your DNA is on the body of Allen Turpin. Albert Johnson you are charged with the murder of Allen Turpin!' Detective Collins declared dramatically. The detective pressed a button on the black box, ending the interview.

***

Pat and Maeve were in the Café savouring afternoon tea of clotted cream, raspberry jam and tea. Maeve sipped her tea whilst Pat tucked into his cream scone. She picked up her new toy, her new smartphone, like an eager child. She touched the screen delicately.

'Check your smartphone Pat.'

Pat put down his scone and picked up his smartphone. He read the text message. The message read: I love you. His eyes welled up.

'Look at the emoji Pat!'

'A heart shaped emoji Maeve!' he laughed with tears in his eyes.

'That was awful Pat being in the maze at the same time as that evil man abducted the boy. 'She reached over and held his hand. 'You're not alone in the maze Pat.'

Sad but brilliant

Pat's mind is like a maze too

The Pharmacist
(A True Story)

'Terence Macswiney is dead!' declared Michael O'Dempsey. 'Starved himself to death in Brixton prison!'

'There'll be trouble,' replied Bill. 'The mob will be making something out of it for sure.'

Bill Kennedy ran the local pharmacy in the small town of Borris, county Carlow, Ireland. A successful businessman, he had a high opinion of himself. Others saw him as insufferably arrogant. Coupled with his bloody-mindedness, he never yielded to anybody. He was a tall man with a ruddy face. His friend Michael O'Dempsey, by contrast was a small, neatly dressed man. His neat appearance was consistent with his profession, a solicitor. They were sitting in the office, located at the back of the pharmacy.

Ireland in 1920 was in tumult. Britain ruled Ireland and would not tolerate any dissent. A political force emerged in Ireland, The Irish Republican Army, demanding an independent Ireland. They took up arms and organised a revolt against British rule. But like David versus Goliath, they were dwarfed by the mighty British empire. Across Ireland Royal Irish Constabulary barracks were attacked by the IRA. Hundreds of RIC barracks, abandoned by the IRC, were burned down by the IRA. As a result of this armed resistance the government dispatched a quasi-military force to Ireland called the Black and Tans to crush the resistance.

Terence Macswiney was the mayor of Cork and an important figure in the Irish Republican Army. His death would trigger a chain of events in one area of Ireland that would lead to tragedy.

***

Eight ghostly figures moved swiftly against the backdrop of the night, moving logs and tree branches and piling them up across the country road until they covered the width of the road. The night was quiet. One of the men used a horse and cart to transport the logs. He also threw an old table on top of the logs. After finishing their task, the eight men, all local farmers, looked at their handiwork.

'That'll feck up the Black and Tan for a while!' declared Seamus, one of the farmers.

In the distance, Maureen, who lived in a nearby house and ran the local general store, was woken by noise from outside. She went to the window and saw the roadblock and the men standing around it. She knew who the men were.

***

Whelan's pub, located at the end of the high street, was a place where news was exchanged. The owner of the pub was Michael Whelan. A middle-aged, softly spoken man he was an IRA supporter. The clan were in the pub that day. The clan were a group of farmers from the local area who were all fervent IRA supporters. There was the twins, Sean and Eamon, both small and wiry; Donal, a large man, built like an ox; Martin, taciturn and watchful; Aidan, a quiet man who tended to drink heavily; Seamus, a talkative man who loved reading the newspaper and expressed his opinions forcefully.

'Yah heard the news?' inquired Michael.

'Your man Macswiney, the mayor of Cork, is dead,' replied Seamus downing his drink.

'A great man sure,' declared Donal.

'A great man, a great Cork man!' agreed Sean.

'A great Irishman. He died for Ireland, like Pearse, Connolly and Clarke before him,' asserted Aidan. At that Seamus held up his drink and everyone sitting around the bar also held up their drink. 'Did you hear what the Black and Tans did in Trim?'

'No,' said Donal.

'Well the IRA burnt down the RIC barracks so in retaliation they sent in two hundred Black and Tans,' said Seamus.

'Two hundred Black and Tans… by Jaysus!' exclaimed Eamon.

'They singled out the shops and businesses that were sympathetic to Sinn Fein. They set fire to the drapery shop and the mineral water factory!' continued Seamus. All the men sitting around the bar were aghast. Aidan interjected.

'There's a hotel there, Higgins's hotel I think it's called?'

'They were given three minutes to get out, then the Black and Tans burned it down!' Seamus replied. 'They set the town hall ablaze. A tailor living nearby came out of his house and was asked where his Sinn Fein sons were. He replied he did not know. A bayonet was placed against his chest and a Black and Tan said put it through the beggar. A postman begged the Black and Tan to spare the old man. They then smashed the door down and smashed up his house. Most of the houses on Market Street were burnt down. People fled their houses screaming. Two young men were shot, they survived their injuries.'

'Bastards!' exclaimed Sean.

'Macswiney didn't die in vain, he didn't starve himself for nothing,' said Aidan.

At that moment the door to the pub opened and a young man wearing a brown tunic and a black pair of trousers, together with a holster containing a gun walked through the door. As an auxiliary officer, Dave patrolled the village of Borris. He was originally attracted to the position of an auxiliary officer by the offer of ten shillings a day, plus a daily supply of cigarettes. The locals treated him with suspicion, but he had a job to do and was unconcerned as to whether he was loved or hated. He had a surly manner and behind this was a natural aggression, an essential asset in an auxiliary officer.

Everybody in the pub turned and looked momentarily at the

Black and Tan. He walked to the bar cocky and confident.

'Whisky please governor,' he said to Michael. 'So I hear your hero Terence Macswiney has died in Brixton prison.'

Michael nodded and gave him his drink and Dave handed him the money. Dave continued his monologue.

'Still don't worry lads because when he goes to heaven the 4th Earl of Sandwich will be there to give him some sandwiches!' He said this with a malicious smile.

The others in the pub, clearly angered by this comment, held their tongue. Dave finished his drink and sensing an atmosphere decided to leave. Making his way to the pub door Donal blurted out the following remark.

'The cowshite on my shoe smells better than any Black and Tan!

Dave heard the comment, ignored it and took his leave.

***

Dave was doing his patrols around Borris when he decided to visit the pharmacy.

'Hello there,' Bill Kennedy pronounced as Dave entered the pharmacy.

'I've got a bit of a cough chemist, can you help me out?'

'Hold on there,' he said.

Bill disappeared through a door to an adjacent room and then re-appeared with a small bottle. Bill and Dave were alone in the pharmacy.

'Just follow the instructions on the bottle,' he continued.

He handed the bottle to Dave. When Dave went to pay Bill waved his hand. 'On the house.'

'Last night there was a roadblock erected just outside town. Hear anything about that? Dave inquired.

'Not a whisper. But I did hear that the local IRA are monitoring the movements of RIC patrols. They know that an RIC patrol passes through the road north of Borris every morning at ten o'clock. They are planning to attack that patrol tomorrow morning,' said Bill.

'Thanks for that,' said Dave.

At that Dave took his leave. As he left the pharmacy Michael Whelan, walking along the road, noted the Black and Tans' departure from the pharmacy.

***

Sean and Eamon, twins, inherited the farm when their father passed away (their mother had died ten years earlier of a blood disorder). They shared the various jobs on the farm. That morning Eamon was in the barn, milking a cow, whilst talking to Sean. The barn floor was strewn with hay and in some areas faeces. A meeting was called and as a result they were joined by Aidan, Seamus, Donal, Martin, and Michael. Everybody stood in the barn, except Eamon, who stopped milking the cow when the others entered the barn.

'Yesterday the brigade sent a unit to attack the RIC patrol just outside Borris. The RIC patrol always passes that piece of road at ten o'clock, but yesterday it didn't happen,' declared Seamus.

'Somebody in the town has been talking to the RIC or the Black and Tans…' stated Donal.

'We'll all have to be careful…' asserted Seamus.

'The other day I saw Black and Tan Dave come out of the pharmacy!' said Michael.

'That fecking eejit Kennedy… he's been blabbing to the Black and Tan!' said Martin.

'Macswiney's funeral is coming up,' said Aidan. 'All the shops will have to close.'

'Including the pharmacy. Kennedy will have to close the shop as a mark of respect!' declared Martin.

'I'll pay Bill Kennedy a visit tomorrow,' said Seamus ominously.

***

Father Quinlivan's' arthritis was playing up. The parish priest of The Sacred heart of Jesus church, had arthritis in his left knee and sometimes it was particularly severe. That morning he had decided to talk to Bill Kennedy, the owner of the pharmacy. He had heard that Kennedy had decided not to close the pharmacy on the day of Terence Macswiney's funeral. He was going to talk to him, with the aim of changing his mind.

He entered the pharmacy and was greeted by Bill Kennedy.

'Good morning, Father Quinlivan. What can I do for you?' he inquired.

'Good morning, Bill. I heard that you were keeping the pharmacy open on the day of Terence Macswiney's funeral?'

'That's right,' he replied defiantly.

'Don't you think you should re-consider your decision? After all a lot of people in this town regard Macswiney as a martyr?'

'Thank you for your advice, Father Quinlivan but on the thirty-first of October this pharmacy will remain open!' Bill Kennedy declared this with absolute certainty.

Father Kennedy, in pain with his arthritis, and Bill Kennedy, stood looking at each other, the gulf between them unable to be bridged. nervous for Bill

'Good day to you,' said Father Quinlivan, conceding defeat. Then he took his leave.

***

'He'll get his comeuppance one day!'

That's what one neighbour said of Bill Kennedy. Arrogant, obstinate, bad tempered, uncompromising he was all these things.

He smoked heavily and liked a drink. He liked horse-riding. A confirmed bachelor he liked the good things in life.

After completing his pharmacy training, he took over the job at the pharmacy. He used to tell his fellow students at college that one day he was going to be well off.

He was a pragmatist. England ruled Ireland. Fact. Every Irishman and Irishwoman had to accept that fact. He dismissed the dreamers who wanted an independent Ireland. If he had to do a deal with the IRC to get on, then so be it.

Bill Kennedy's pharmacy interior was framed by a long wooden shelf behind which stood various glass cabinets containing bottles of medicine. The pharmacy was dominated by a large cabinet containing multiple small compartments.

Through the window Bill Kennedy could see the farmer advancing toward the pharmacy. He knew what this was about, and he was determined to hold his ground. Seamus entered the pharmacy.

'Good morning,' said Seamus politely.

'Good morning,' replied Bill.

'Yah heard that Terence Macswiney died?' inquired Seamus.

'I did sure,' said Bill.

'Well all the shops in Borris will be closing on the day of his funeral on the thirty-first of October as a mark of respect,' declared Seamus.

'Now listen…' Bill did not know his name.

'Seamus.'

'Seamus. I have no legal obligation to close the pharmacy on that day, so I shall be remaining open,' Bill said with complete composure.

An uncomfortable silence descended on the pharmacy. The two men were now at loggerheads.

'Yah know that every Irishman has a choice to make. Every Irishman must choose. You are either for the RIC and the Black and Tans or against them,' declared Seamus.

Bill Kennedy did not respond to this. Seamus took his leave.

***

The sacred Heart of Jesus church had a granite façade. It had two arch-shaped windows above a Romanesque doorway. The church service, in memory of Terence Macswiney, was full, people standing at the back of the church. It was the thirty-first of October 1920, the date of Patrick Macswiney's funeral. In Cork Macswiney's funeral service was carried out at the Cathedral of St. Mary and St. Anne. His coffin was draped in the colours of Sinn Fein, the political wing of the IRA.

Father Quinlivan presided over the church service. With his lined face and slight stoop, he was a familiar figure in Borris. Aidan, Seamus, Sean, Eamon, Donal, Martin, Michael, were sitting in the pews, listening intently. Bill Kennedy was noticeably absent. Father Quinlivan delivered a few words about Terence Macswiney.

'Terence Macswiney deliberately starved himself to death in Brixton prison after he was arrested for sedition by the British government. This is a time of crisis for Ireland. Many see him as a martyr for Ireland. Every Irish man and Irish woman should remember Terence Macswiney's words: it is not those who can inflict the most, but those who can suffer the most who will prevail.'

When the church service finished everybody filed out. The clan gathered outside the church.

'The pharmacy is still open!' declared Donal.

They all looked at one another, seething with anger.

'If Kennedy thinks this is the end of the matter, he is very mistaken,' declared Seamus ominously.

***

The clan gathered at Whelan's pub. They all sat around the bar drinking their beer, still seething with anger. There was no one else in the pub.

'I've told the vice-commandant of the 4th brigade about your man consorting with the Black and Tan…' said Seamus quietly.

'What about a boycott of the pharmacy,' said Donal.

They all looked at each other.

'Great idea Donal!' said Eamon.

'Good,' affirmed Seamus. 'We need to speak to everybody in the area and tell them to boycott Kennedy's pharmacy!'

'I'll start talking to my neighbours today,' declared Martin.

'We'll do the same!' said Eamon speaking for both himself and his brother.

'Most people will go along with the boycott,' asserted Aidan.

'We'll make life impossible for that fecker!' declared Seamus.

***

Maureen Rooney ran the general store in Borris. A middle-aged, warm-hearted woman she had run the shop for five years, taking it over after her father died. She now managed everything: stock, accounts and service delivery. The shopfront had a green façade and above was the name Rooney, coloured in yellow. Whenever a Black and Tan came into the shop, she managed to bury her hatred for them beneath a veneer of politeness.

She was stocking Irish cigarettes on the shelf when Seamus entered the shop. He was limping, because of being kicked by one of his cattle. Seamus and Maureen knew each other well. Seamus' father was friends with Maureen's father.

'Have you come in here to stir the pot?' Maureen asked bluntly.

'Now Maureen I'm not stirring the pot. Bill Kennedy is stirring the pot. We're asking everybody to boycott his pharmacy. He refused to close his shop on the day of Terence Macswiney's funeral for God's sake!'

'I know. Fine. I'll boycott the pharmacy. But Seamus you've got to promise me one thing. That nothing happens to Michael O'Dempsey! He's a good man.'

'Good men love Ireland!' Seamus replied sharply.

'Michael loves Ireland,' declared Maureen.

'Does he?' said Seamus, his reply ringing with doubt. 'If he loves Ireland why is he friends with Bill Kennedy?'

At that Seamus took his leave. Maureen stared at Seamus' huge frame as he walked out of the shop limping.

The following day Michael O'Dempsey entered the shop. Always perfectly dressed, his suit was cut by a tailor in Wexford. His manners matched his clothes; they were exact and precise. Every week he came into Maureen's shop for some cigarettes. Maureen's soft heart softened further when she saw Michael O'Dempsey. But Michael O'Dempsey did not share those romantic feelings.

'Good morning, Maureen, a packet of cigarettes and the newspaper please,' he said picking up the newspaper from the counter.

'There,' she replied handing him the cigarettes.

He handed her the money, knowing the exact amount required as these were his regular purchases.

'Seamus was in yesterday,' she said.

'Was he. And what did he want?' he replied.

'He wants everybody in the town to boycott the pharmacy,' she declared.

'What!' he said in astonishment. 'The bloody cheek!' Who does he think he is!

'The people in the town will follow his lead,' she asserted confidently.

'Thanks Maureen. 'He picked up his cigarettes from the counter and turned to leave.

'Michael,' Maureen sounded earnest. 'Be careful. Your friendship with Bill Kennedy may cost you dear!'

Michael O'Dempsey stared at Maureen after she made this dramatic statement, remained silent then took his leave.

Maureen's main hobby was painting. Some of her work was displayed on the walls of her shop. But the painting that was dear to her heart was displayed on the wall of her living room. The painting featured the viaduct that was located just beyond Borris railway station. The viaduct had thirteen arches. Maureen had worked hard on the painting and was proud of it. Underneath one of the arches were two figures, a couple holding hands. Maureen secretly imagined that the couple was herself and Michael O'Dempsey.

***

Michael O'Dempseys' office resembled a legal office straight out of the pages of a Charles Dickens story. One wall was covered by three shelves; they were stuffed with legal texts pronouncing on this and that issue. On the opposite wall were three shelves full of legal documents, leases and so forth, each document tied up with a ribbon. A large wooden desk filled the centre of the room. Michael was sitting at his desk, studying a document when Bill Kennedy stormed into the room.

'Bill!' said Michael, looking up from his document, with some alarm at the figure in front of him.

'Who does he think he is!' Bill Kennedy declared.

'Who are you talking about?' inquired Michael looking confused.

'Your man Seamus… he paid me a visit yesterday,' Bill replied.

‘What did he want?

‘He came to deliver a message. That I’m to stop upsetting the apple cart. That I’m to do as I’m told!’ declared Bill.

‘Well Maureen in the general store tells me that the clan are organising a boycott of your pharmacy,’ said Michael.

‘A boycott! Bastards!’ Bill erupted at the sound of the word. ‘I want to take out an injunction against the bastards. All of them!’

‘Against all of them!’ said Michael.

‘Absolutely!’ affirmed Bill.

‘Well I’ll have to apply to the High Court,’ said Michael in full solicitor mode. ‘The injunction will have to be specific.’

‘They’re not to step inside the pharmacy and they’re not to come within a hundred feet of my house!’ Bill declared with certainty.

‘Maybe Bill you should find some common ground with these people… come to some sort of agreement?’ inquired Michael.

‘Common ground?’ Bill replied with incredulity. ‘Are yah dreaming?’

‘If you do this it will raise the temperature all around,’ cautioned Michael, adopting the tone of a solicitor.

‘A line has been crossed. There’s no going back now,’ Bill said.

‘Are you sure Bill you want to do this?’ inquired Michael.

‘I’m one hundred per cent sure,’ he declared.

‘I’ll get the particulars of the men, full names, addresses and then I’ll apply to the High Court for an injunction. ‘Michael paused. ‘You may win in a legal court but in the court of public opinion you will lose Bill. The people of the town are against you!’

‘Feck ’em!’ Bill Kennedy was now set on a path of total defiance.

***

Berna Laverty was a fun loving, sixteen-year-old country girl with bundles of energy who helped her father with various tasks on his farm. She helped him feed the pigs and milk the cows. With her friends she often practised Irish dancing in the evening.

She entered the general store to get some provisions. She picked up bread, tea, sugar, biscuits and cigarettes for her beloved father. Maureen greeted her warmly.

'How's' your dad Berna?' inquired Maureen.

'Fine thanks Maureen,' said Berna.

'You know that there's a boycott against the pharmacy?' inquired Maureen.

'No, I didn't,' said Berna.

'Your man refused to close the pharmacy on the day of Terence Macswiney's funeral. I don't go in there anymore,' said Maureen clarifying the matter.

'Well I won't be going in there then,' Berna said. She paid for her purchases and left.

As she left the shop and walked down the high street, she came across a Black and Tan officer, Dave. On his patrols he saw her working on her farm. It was clear he took a shine to her. Whenever she saw him, she neither encouraged him nor rebuffed him. He smiled at her as they met in the street.

'How's' the pigs on the farm?' he inquired.

'Fine thanks,' she replied.

'What a waste! A beautiful girl like you feeding pigs!' he remarked dismissively. She laughed. He produced a bar of chocolate from his pocket. He handed the bar of chocolate to her. 'Here take this. Good luck. 'He then took his leave.

She was about to continue walking when suddenly a man behind her called her name. It was Michael who managed the pub.

She stopped.

'Berna… remember the Black and Tan are no friends of Ireland. And Black and Tan Dave is no friend of yours!'

'Ok Michael,' she replied.

'Say hello to your dad,' he said and then he took his leave.

***

At the end of a field owned by Eamon and Sean there was an area called the Bog, an area consisting of peat. They were cutting the turf. This entailed cutting oblong pieces of turf and then putting them out to dry. Eamon and Sean took turns cutting the turf with a spade and loading it on to a wheelbarrow. Eamon's hobby was reading, and this often-provoked banter between the two brothers.

'Have you learnt any new words in all the reading yah do?' inquired Sean.

'Well, sure, I have. 'Eamon stopped cutting the turf for a moment. 'The spade I'm using to cut the turf would generally be called an implement.'

'An implement,' repeated Sean.

'That's right, as in tool. But implement has a second meaning. The other meaning is to carry out something, as in to implement a plan,' said Eamon.

'Implement… sounds like inclement,' said Sean.

'Totally different word. Inclement refers to the weather…' said Eamon.

But his train of thought was interrupted by the sight of a group of men advancing toward them. Seamus, Donal, Aidan, and Michael stopped when they came upon the brothers.

'Ah the smell of turf!' exclaimed Seamus.

'What's up?' inquired Eamon.

'I've heard a whisper that your man Kennedy has told his

solicitor O'Dempsey to take out an injunction against all ten of us!' Seamus declared vehemently.

'An injunction? What does that mean? inquired Sean.

'It means we won't be able to set foot in his pharmacy or go near his house,' said Donal.

'Bastard!' exclaimed Eamon.

'What shall we do?' asked Martin.

'Well I believe Michael O'Dempsey's office is in Enniscorthy, Wexford. So, we'll break into his office and steal the legal papers!' declared Seamus.

'Right so!' said Sean.

'We'll do it at a weekend when everything is quiet,' said Seamus.

'I volunteer!' said Martin.

'Fine. Just the two of us. We'll do it this weekend!' declared Seamus.

***

Maureen was unable to sleep. She thought of her late mother. An indelible image: making breakfast for her late father in the kitchen, lavishing butter on his toast. She got up and went downstairs. She opened the front door and looked out at the country road and the fields opposite, enveloped in darkness and silence.

The sleepy rhythm of life in Boriss was disturbed by the currents of tension rippling through Ireland. Recently the IRA had burned down RIC barracks in nearby Milford. Now there was the stand-off between Bill Kennedy, the pharmacist, and the clan (the IRA). Entangled in this stand-off was the object of Maureen's dreams and affection, Michael O'Dempsey.

Suddenly the silence of the night was broken by the sound of approaching hooves. Out of the darkness appeared a runaway: a runaway horse. It galloped majestically and mysteriously past Maureen's house and then disappeared into the night.

Maureen felt it was an omen.

***

Bill Kennedy lived in a comfortable house on the edge of town. It was the family home handed down to him when his parents passed away. Bill answered the front door; it was his friend and solicitor Michael O'Dempsey. He looked pale and shaken. Bill invited him.

'Michael. Come in.'

Michael was motioned into the living room.

'My office has been broken into! All the legal papers relating to the injunction have been stolen!' he declared.

Bill Kennedy seethed with anger. He paced backward and forward, unable to contain his anger.

'That gang of bastards!' he shouted.

'Do you want to continue with this?' inquired Michael O'Dempsey.

'Definitely! Draw up another set of legal papers… the injunction will go ahead!' he said defiantly.

'Are you sure?' Michael inquired.

'I'm sure,' Bill replied decisively. 'Come here. I want to show you something.'

Bill walked into the kitchen and Michael followed him. There was a large cabinet containing shelves of dishes and cups. At the bottom of the cabinet were two drawers. Bill knelt and opened the last drawer and removed a box. He put the box on the kitchen table and opened it. The box contained a pistol, plus rounds of ammunition. Michael looked startled when he saw the pistol.

'My father handed down this pistol. With rounds of ammunition. 'Bill paused. 'A man must stand his ground. From now on I'm arming myself when I go out!'

Michael stood and stared at his friend and then took his leave.

Later that night, as Bill drifted off to sleep, he was sure he heard something downstairs. He leapt out of bed and rushed downstairs, picking up his gun from the bedside table. He was sure an intruder had penetrated the privacy of his home. He searched the front and rear of the house but found nothing. Eventually he went back to bed.

Bill Kennedy was now a creature haunted by fearful thoughts. Watchful, hyper alert, suspicious, wary, anxious he was all these things. His nerves were constantly frayed. One evening he paced to and fro in his living room, gun in hand, staring out of the window to the street outside. He knew that one day the clan would come for him.

The next day Bill Kennedy started carrying a gun around with him. He took it to work. He carried it around with him when he walked through the town. He wore a suit to work and carried the gun in his inside pocket. He was determined to defend himself. He would not be beaten. He would not be defeated.

One day, after finishing work at the pharmacy, he walked home as usual to his house on the edge of town. It was a quiet day, the streets nearly empty. But he was aware of somebody walking behind him. He turned around and saw it was one of the clan, Donal. Bill Kennedy was being followed.

The same thing happened the next day. Bill noted that it was Donal following him again. The street was empty, just him and Donal. This time Bill snapped. He pulled out his gun. It was loaded. He fired the gun at the ground, to the left of Donal, a warning shot. Donal looked stunned; he froze. Donal stopped and beat a hasty retreat. Donal reported the incident to his friends in the clan.

***

The viaduct, with its multiple arches, stood majestically against the skyline. The viaduct injected a sweeping sense of drama into the landscape. Seamus had been summoned to a meeting by the vice commandant of Carlows' 4th brigade. He waited at the base of one of the arches, dwarfed by this immense structure. He had been waiting five minutes when he saw a tall figure striding toward him. It was the vice commandant. They shook hands.

'Commander,' said Seamus.

'Seamus,' said the vice commandant. He had steady eyes and a firm handshake. 'You've heard what happened in Cork. The Black and Tans burnt down the town hall and the Corn Exchange!'

'Bastards!'

'Ireland is on fire Seamus and the Black and Tans are starting the fire. 'The vice commandant paused. 'So is your man the pharmacist consorting with The Black and Tans?'

'Definitely!' declared Seamus. 'We're sure he's passing on information to the Black and Tans. And last evening he fired a shot at Donal out in the street!'

'He's armed! Was Donal hurt?'

'No. Donal said it was a warning shot,' said Seamus.

'And what about the solicitor O'Dempsey?' inquired the vice commandant.

'He issued the injunctions to me, Donal and the others. Him and Kennedy are as thick as thieves. I'm sure he's also passing on information to the Black and Tans!' asserted Seamus.

'The town is quiet of an evening?' inquired the vice commandant.

'Yes,' said Seamus.

'I want you to monitor their movements, find out when they are alone together,' said the vice commandant calmly.

'Right,' said Seamus. 'What will you do?'

'We are at war against the British empire. Look what happened on the twenty-first of November, a couple of months ago in Dublin? Twelve agents of the British state, soldiers, RIC officers, informers were killed on the orders of Michael Collins himself. British blood wiil flow and Irish blood will flow. Informers will be crushed Seamus,' said the vice commandant ominously, the steely glint in his eyes all too apparent.

***

It was a cool March evening in the town of Borris. Bill Kennedy was conducting an inventory of his stock when he was visited by his solicitor and friend Michael O'Dempsey. Bill invited his friend to his house for alcoholic refreshments. They decided to bypass any local pubs as there was still a tense atmosphere in the town and sometimes downright hostility. The town was enveloped in darkness as they walked toward Bill Kennedy's house. The street was empty. They were totally unaware that two armed men lay in wait nearby.

Then suddenly, emerging out of an alleyway, two men appeared. Michael saw them first. He could see that they both held an object in their hands, the object pointing to the ground. Then both men simultaneously raised their arms. As soon as Bill Kennedy saw the two men raise their arms, he knew he was dead.

The two men fired their weapons. They discharged several shots that hit the two targets. Bill Kennedy died instantly; Michael O'Dempsey died later of his wounds. The two assassins disappeared into the night.

***

The family of Michael O'Dempsey made representations to the Irish government proclaiming his innocence. In February 1922 the Free State government granted his mother financial compensation and acknowledged that he wasn't a spy.

Intense

Old Tom
(A True Story)

'Bless me father for I have sinned it is two months since my last confession. IRA command decided we had to execute an informer. Then I used the dead body of the informer for a military operation… the war drives you to do terrible things Father. God forgive me.'

Through the grill of the confession box, amidst the darkness, Father Grogan could see the outline of a head. The Father knew who was talking; it was Captain Manson Moyniham of the Irish Republican Army.

***

'Bless me Father for I have sinned it is a month since my last confession… Father I have done a terrible thing… we had our orders… we are fighting for Ireland… I executed a spy. Two weeks earlier I slaughtered a sheep on the farm. Now I had to slaughter a human being Father. We blindfolded your man. I couldn't look at his eyes. We aimed for his heart. It was quick. He died instantly. I fired my rifle, he slumped to the ground and he was dead. Will God forgive me Father?'

Through the grill of the confession box Father Grogan could see the outline of a head. It was Pat, a local farmer and member of Rathmore's IRA unit. Pat's confession had come hard on the heels of Manus Moynihan's confession. This was no coincidence.

***

Three weeks earlier. 1920's Ireland was being torn apart by violence. Ireland was under the thumb of the British Empire. Armed insurrection emerged in the form of the IRA. Royal Irish

Constabulary barracks across the country were besieged and burnt down by the IRA. As a result the British government sent in a quasi military force, the Black and Tans to bolster security and back up the RIC.

Rathmore, a small village in county Kerry, was caught up in this upheaval. The high street consisted of a number of shops, general stores, a pub and a post office. There was a plinth on the high street on which was was placed a cross made out of stone. The IRA were well established in this area. The local community knew who the volunteers were; and kept silent about this knowledge. They knew they were fighting for the soul of Ireland.

***

Tom O'Sullivan was a traveller and a singer of Irish folk songs. He had an other worldly quality about him. He previously had travelled around Westport in county Mayo, doing farm labouring jobs and singing Irish folk songs in pubs. He had moved through counties Galway and Clare until he had reached county Kerry. He then discovered the small village of Rathmore. He had been walking the sacred earth of Ireland for over eighty years. He had counted himself lucky that he was still able to savour the stars in the night sky.

Around the village of Rathmore he was known as Old Tom. He had become a fixture aound Rathmore. His snow-capped head of hair and white beard were well known to the people of Rathmore. He often said that I roam the roads of Ireland with the words of Irish folk songs floating inside my head. He liked to sing the repertoire of Irish folk songs, Danny Boy, The Fields of Athenry, the Irish Rover and Wild Mountain Thyme. He endeavoured to get on with everybody; but at a time of division and violence this was an impossible task.

At present he was helping out Paddy McGinty with some farm labouring jobs, principally feeding the pigs and a sow.

***

In the background overhead a full moon dominated the night sky. Four men, with shovels, were digging up a remote road around Rathmore. The four men were Manus Moynihan and his fellow IRA volunteers, Mick, Pat and John. The purpose of the exercise was to instil fear in the RIC and Black and Tan patrols, by making them think that the road was mined with explosive.

***

The siege of Tralee was burned into the memories of everybody in Rathmore. At the time they had daily reports about events unfolding in that area. The Black and Tans had effectively cut off Tralee. All businesses were closed. They imposed a curfew. They allowed no food in or out of the town. Two IRA men and two civilians were killed in Ardent by the Black and Tans. The siege lasted seven days.

The Black and Tans instilled fear in the local population by various methods. On the 1st November 1920 they fired at crowds leaving mass at Tralee. Volley after volley of bullets resounded to the terror of the people leaving the church.

The siege of Tralee was a reprisal for a wave of violence unleashed by the IRA. The wrath of the IRA was provoked by two events: first, the death on hunger strike in Brixton prison of the mayor of Cork, Terence Macswiney and second, the execution by hanging of the eighteen-year-old IRA volunteer, Kevin Barry, for his involvement in the murder of three British soldiers in Dublin. Over this period the IRA in Kerry shot sixteen RIC officers; seven were killed. Almost all local magistrates resigned their commission for fear of terrorism.

***

Brady's bar on the high street was a focal point for the exchange of news. Paddy, a stout man in his fifties, ran the bar with cheerful good humour. It was just after midday, so there were only a few people in the bar. Tom O'Sullivan sat in the corner drinking a pint of beer. Gathered around the bar were two farmers, Cyril and

Seamus.

'Yah heard what happened in Abbeydorney?' asked Cyril.

'No,' said Seamus.

'The Black and Tans burned down the creamery!'

'Bastards!'

'People relied on that creamery for their incomes,' said Paddy.

'Well the IRA got their own back when they targeted two Black and Tans who were terrorising the locals in Farranfore. They were on a train. Two IRA men boarded the train and shot them dead in the train carriage,' said Cyril.

'The Black and Tans are the scum of the earth!' declared Paddy.

'Amen to that,' said Seamus.

Tom listened to this conversation intently. Then the door of the bar opened and in walked a tall figure with a solemn expression on his face. All three at the bar recognised the figure who had just entered and treated him with the utmost respect.

'How's the farm Manus?'asked Seamus.

'Good. I'm always busy,' said Manus. 'I'll have a pint of the usual.'

'We were just talking about how the Black and Tans burned down the creamery in Abbeydorney. Put a lot of people out of work,' said Paddy, whilst drawing out the pint of beer.

'Mark my words. The Black and Tan will pay for their evil deeds,' said Manus with a dark glint in his eyes.

The pub fell silent for a minute.

'Tom will yah sing us a song?' asked Paddy.

'Ah do Tom,' said Seamus.

Tom smiled and lifted his glass.

'What about Danny boy?' said Tom.

'Grand,' said Paddy.

'O Danny boy the pipes the pipes are calling from glen to glen and down the mountainside. The summer's gone and all the roses falling. Tis you, tis you must go and I must bide you…'

Cyril, Seamus, Paddy and Manus looked at Tom, his sweet voice bringing a smile to their faces. When he finished the song Manus turned to Paddy and said that man deserves a pint. Paddy pulled the pint and and walked over to Tom's table and gave it to him. At the bar Manus raised his glass to Tom. This was the first time they met.

'Fairplay to yah,' said Manus to Tom.

***

Later that afternoon Tom wandered around the village. He said hello to Maeve who ran the post office. In the distance he saw the Black and Tans barracks. The locals gave this place a wide berth.

Sometimes Tom travelled to Killarney and visited the Black and Tans barracks there. The Black and Tans used foul language and were uncouth. Some of the Black and Tans were ex-criminals. But they always gave him a cup of tea and something to eat. They asked him questions about the locals in Rathmore and he told them what he knew. They wanted to know who were the volunteers for the IRA in Rathmore.

Tom gave them the name of a farmer who he suspected was an IRA volunteer. The Black and Tans raided his farm and ransacked it, looking for weapons. But the search was fruitless; they found nothing. Tom's suspicions were correct however; the farmer was a IRA volunteer but had no weapons, as the Rathmore company of the IRA were short of rifles.

A week later Tom saw the same farmer, Pat, in the village. Pat had no idea that he was engaging in conversation with an informer.

'Hello Tom,' said Pat.

'Morning Pat. How's the farm?'

'Ransacked by the Black and Tans! They turned the place upside down. Smashed a wooden chair. They found nothing of course. Cockney bastards! I'm a law abiding citizen Tom.'

'Sure of course you are. Be seeing you!' said Tom and he took his leave.

Nobody in Rathmore quite realised Tom's true character. They only saw a harmless eccentric.

***

Walking past the Catholic church Tom saw the parish priest Father Grogan. Tom looked in more robust health than Father Grogan whose physical frame was unduly thin. The Father was taking medicine for a heart condition. They greeted each other. Then Father Grogan invited him into his private quarters for some lunch. They walked through the interior of the church, past the ornate altar. The housekeeper was preparing bacon and eggs.

'Sure, that would be lovely Father Grogan,' said Tom.

Tom consumed the meal with relish.

'Well Tom I hear you're helping out Paddy McGinty on his farm?'

'That's right. I feed the pigs and the sow twice a day. I get a meal every day. And I smell the beautiful Irish country air.'

'And I hear your singing your Irish songs in Brady's pub?'

'That's right Father.'

'And I'm pleased that you're a regular at mass.'

'I'm a good Catholic father.'

'You are a good Catholic Tom.'

Then Tom took his leave.

***

Manus Moynihan convened a meeting of his comrades in arms in a barn on his farm. Pat was first to arrive, small and wiry with a ready smile. He was followed by Mick, a heavily built man with a shy demeanor. John and Mick, two large men, smelling heavily of alcohol, followed. They were all standing amongst the hay. Manus looked at Pat.

'Are you ok Pat?'

'I'm fine.'

It was clear that John and Mick were unaware of the raid on Pat's farm.

'My farm was raided yesterday. The Black and Tans found nothing, because we're short of rifles.'

'I think gentlemen we can assume we have an informer in Rathmore,' declared Manus adopting a grave tone. 'There have been informers in Cork. In February a man was shot dead for giving evidence to the crown court. Another informer in Cork was shot last year as a result of being part of a spy ring. So when we find the culprit we will need to take the necessary action. In the mean time be careful.'

All four men exchanged glances and then they took their leave.

***

Occasionally a motor vehicle driven by the Black and Tans would drive through the streets of Rathmore. Manus Moynihan had just purchased some groceries from the general store and was walking along the street, greeting various locals. The motor vehicle had four Black and Tan officers in it when suddenly the silence was broken by the sound of gunshot; a volley of bullets had been discharged into the air. People scurried into doorways. But Manus did not flinch. He remained still. He knew that this was a tactic deployed by the Black and Tans to instil fear in the local population.

It was incidents like this that would explain how a mild mannered farmer became a IRA leader, who could load and unload a rifle with proficiency and could kill an RIC officer or Black and Tan without hesitation. The war of indepence had forged a steel within Manus Moyniham. That steel had given him the courage to take on a military force controlled by an empire that bestrode the world.

***

Every Tuesday Father Grogan held confessions between ten and eleven. Father Grogan waited patiently in the dark of the confession box. Somebody entered the confession box.

'Bless me Father for I have sinned it's four months since my last confession.

Father I've done something that is wrong. I've told the Black and Tan officers things about the locals.'

There was a long pause.

'Say the act of contrition,' said Father Grogan.

'My God I am sorry for my sins with all my heart and with your help I am willing to do penance.'

'I absolve you of your sins in the name of the Father, the Son and the Holy Spirit.'

Then the person exited the confession box. The confession box was sealed and a priest could not divulge to anybody anything that was said in the confession box. Father Grogan recognised the man's voice: it was old Tom.

***

Father Grogan noticed that Manus Moynihan was sitting in the pew in the church. Father Grogan was aware of his IRA status. They greeted each other, then he sat next to Manus.

'We have an informer in our midst Father!' declared Manus.

'Oh God.'

'Any ideas who it is?'

'Sorry Manus, no.'

'Keep your ear to the ground and let me know if you hear anything.'

'I will so.'

Then Manus took his leave.

***

Manus Moynihan wanted to keep the RIC and the Black and Tans on their toes, so he decided to do some sniping at the RIC barracks. The Rathmore RIC barracks, consisting of a two storey house built of stone, was located opposite the railway station. Armed with a rifle (the only rifle Rathmore company had) he took up a position where he could make a speedy retreat. He discharged a number of shots at the windows of the barracks; return fire did not come close to hurting him. There were no confirmed casualties. He then made a swift exit. The Black and Tans did not pursue him; they were too afraid of being drawn into an ambush.

***

Manus Moynihan convened a meeting in his barn. John, Pat. Denis and Mick were all there. He was pacing backwards and forwards; he was clearly excited.

'Good news. The IRA carried out a successful ambush at Headford Junction railway station on the 21st March. A group of British soldiers, coming from Kenmare, were getting off at Headford Junction. The Kerry unit had taken up position in the station. When the soldiers got off the Kerry unit opened fire. The soldiers didn't know what hit them. Eight British soldiers were killed. Unfortunately we lost two of the Kerry unit and two civilians were killed.'

'A great result!' declared Pat.

'Sure after this the Black and Tans and RIC will be more reluctant to do patrols in the countryside. They'll be fearful of an ambush!' said Mick.

'You're right Mick. We'll have to think of ways of drawing them out of their barracks,' said Manus.

Mick's prediction that the RIC and the Black and Tans would stop their patrols in the countryside proved correct.

***

Old Tom was wandering around the Rathmore countryside, singing aloud the Irish folk song Wild Rover. The sky was clear, the sun shining. Up ahead he saw a horse drawn carriage, parked on the side of the road. A woman emerged from the carriage and greeted him when he approached. She wore a shawl around her shoulders.

'You're a traveller?'

'I am sure. Like yourself.'

'Did you come from Rathmore?'

'I did. A grand place.'

'I'm Sarah.'

'I'm Tom.'

She looked at Tom intensely.

'Beware Tom. Ireland is ripping itself apart. You will be used by both sides, the Black and Tans and the IRA. Mark my words.'

'Sarah, I'm a child of nature. I sing my songs and don't take sides in these great struggles. Good luck.'

'Good luck Tom.'

He continued walking along the country lane.

***

Manus Moynihan was a paid a visit by Eddie Crowley, whose brother was an active volunteer with the Rathmore company. Eddie reported that he had been arrested by the Black and Tans in Killarney and had been detained in the RIC barracks there. He had just been released. Whilst in custody there he saw an old man visiting the Black and Tans regularly. The man was called old Tom. It was within the realm of possibility that Tom, being a traveller, travelled regularly between Killarney and Rathmore.

As a result Tom was picked up by a unit of the IRA on the Cork border and detained by the IRA. Just after this two British army deserters, tired and frightened, were picked up by a unit of the IRA. When questioned they had evidence pertaining to old Tom. They too told Manus Moynihan that they had seen a man referred to as old Tom visiting the Black and Tans in the barracks in Killarney. They later identified old Tom as Tom O'Sullivan.

Events slowly unfolded toward an inevitable conclusion. An IRA court was set up to try old Tom. The court consisted of six members of the IRA, including Manus Moynihan. Manus looked at Tom and recalled that he had heard him singing Danny Boy in Brady's bar a while ago. But he pushed this memory out of his head. His heart had turned to stone. Under questioning Tom was evasive and denied that he visited the Black and Tans. The court took evidence from Eddie Crowley and the two British army deserters.

The court was not swayed by Tom's age or look of wounded innocence. The court was unmoved by his statement that 'I'm just an innocent traveller, wandering here and there'. The court found him guilty of spying and the sentence was execution by firing squad. This was war and any vestige of humanity had vanished.

Manus Moynihan would arrange the execution. Three IRA volunteers would form the firing squad. The rifles would be obtained from other Kerry units. Old Tom would be executed near the Bog road just outside Rathmore. Manus Moynihan had to return to his farm briefly, to sort out the manure on his farm. He then returned and gave the order to carry out the execution. Old Tom said nothing in his last minutes on earth. He was killed by three bullets.

After the execution Manus was reminded of something that Mick said. That the Black and Tans were reluctant to go out on patrols to the countryside. A thought occurred to Manus. Position

Tom's corpse on the Bog road as bait, to draw out the Black and Tans. His IRA comrades agreed with the idea, although privately Mick was appalled by the idea. Mick and John carried Tom's corpse to the Bog road and laid it down in the middle of the road. A sheet of paper was attached to the corpse. It said: Convicted as a Spy.

***

The Bog road was a curved road, bordered by hedges, that intersected with a boreen (a small country lane). The hedges were high, providing good cover for an IRA unit. Manus regarded the Bog road as the perfect spot for an ambush. Manus talked it over with other units in the Kerry and Cork areas and they decided to mass forces off the Bog road. A total of fifty IRA volunteers gathered, armed to the teeth.

Whilst waiting the IRA units observed a man driving a donkey and cart approach the Bog road. The IRA officers were instructed to maintain complete silence. When he came across the dead body the man stopped and stared at this ghoulish scene. He decided to return to Rathmore and report this to the RIC. The old man had not seen the IRA officers hiding behind the hedges. The IRA units watched him return to Rathmore.

On receiving the news that there was a dead body on a remote road in Rathmore the RIC officers proclaimed that this was a hoax. They were then taunted, by their Black and Tan colleagues, who accused them of being cowards. The upshot was that nine Black and Tan officers, in two motor vehicles, headed for the Bog road.

When Manus saw the two vehicles approach the Bog road he knew his plan had succeeded. The two vehicles stopped at the corpse of Tom O'Sullivan. The nine Black and Tan officers got out of their vehicles, whereupon the IRA, watching nervously, waiting for the order to open fire, pulled the triggers of their rifles. Taken completely by surprise, almost all of the Black and Tans officers were killed. Eight Black and Tan officers were killed; one escaped. Eight rifles were seized, plus eight hundred rounds of ammunition.

The IRA officers, in large numbers, milled around the dead

Black and Tan officers. Manus, Mick, John and Pat walked to the corpse of old Tom and stood over him. Manus looked down.

'In life he betrayed Ireland. In death he served Ireland,' declared Manus.

Well, damn!

Insects

'Do you like insects?' inquired the little girl.

Darting eyes in an angelic face dominated by a sweeping smile the little girl had stopped Mary, a plump twenty-five-year-old worker at Talbots supermarket. Twelve-year-old Veronica was out shopping with her mother who was in a queue for customer services; the supermarket was quite busy.

'Do I like insects,' smiled Mary taken aback by the question. 'Well to be honest their very small and I don't think about them much… but I like ladybirds!'

'Their orange!' she replied her eyes blazing with excitement.

'There are lots of different types of insects… ants, bees, cockroaches, centipedes…' Mary said racking her brains to think of all the different categories.

'Moths!' the little girl declared with unrestrained excitement. 'Have you ever rode a bicycle on a bumpy road?'

'Well… no I haven't actually,' Mary replied startled by the question.

At that moment her mother left the queue and re-joined her daughter. The little girl waved at Mary as she exited the store. Talbots supermarket was a large supermarket, occupying a vast space. High ceilings looked down on row upon row of products ranging from foodstuffs, cleaning materials to clothes. Mary worked on the self-service section with her friend Daphne, a tall broad shouldered young woman distinguished by her Goth make-up. They both shared an unlimited curiosity about other people and had a vivid imagination. Their imaginations were nourished in the main by popualr culture. Their cultural reference points were the X-Files, Buffy The Vampire Slayer and Star Trek. Mary also had a liking for film versions of Dickens, particularly Great Expectations.

They both took a break in the staff canteen. There were news reports on the TV that a twelve-year-old boy had gone missing in the local area.

'They still haven't found that boy who's gone missing,' remarked Daphne.

'No, poor thing,' replied Mary. At that moment a tall, thin young man approached their table. Henry was what some people would describe as a nerd and possessed a repertoire of obscure knowledge. He had a tendency to ask questions that only he could answer. This afforded him great pleasure.

'Afternoon ladies,' he said breezily sitting next to them. 'And how's things on self-service?'

'Busy,' replied Mary.

'Well I have a question for you. What is entomology?' he asked his face beaming. Mary and Daphne looked at each other puzzled. 'Well it's a branch of zoology that's given over to the study of insects.'

'Well it's funny you should mention insects because today a girl asked me if I liked insects.' At this Daphne jumped in.

'Did you see that old film last night on TV… The Naked Jungle with Charlton Heston?'

'Wow… yeah. Brilliant.' At this she turned to Henry. 'What is Marabunta?' The smile disappeared from his face; he had clearly never heard of the word.

'I don't know,' he replied crestfallen. Mary had brilliantly turned the tables on him.

'Marabunta means an army of ants on the move who destroy everything in its path. Charlton Heston plays a plantation owner in South America who's threatened by an army of ants.'

'So it's Charlton Heston versus an army of ants… got it,' said Henry.

'Exactly.'

'So how does he defeat the ants?' inquired Henry.

'He floods the area around the plantation and wipes out the ants,' replied Mary.

'But get this… as the the army of ants are advancing through the jungle they send out a scout…' Excited Mary jumps in and interrupts Daphne.

'That's right. An advanced guard to check out the area. That's intelligence for you!'

At that one of their colleagues, Brenda, passed the table. She approached Mary and bent over.

'There's ants in the Ladies toilet!' she declared. Mary, Daphne and Henry looked at each other.

'Marabunta!' declared Daphne.

***

The music spread over the length and breadth of Talbot's.

'I just can't get you out of my head

Boy your loving is all I think about

I just can't get you out of my head.'

Mary and Daphne had worked at Talbot's supermarket a number of years and got to know the regular customers. One of these customers was an elegant older lady, a retired barrister. Always beautifully dressed she displayed exquisite old world manners. Contrary to the stereotype of the elegant, clever barrister she was friendly although this was counter balanced by a sinister smile.

'There's Mrs Roberts,' observed Daphne.

'Always elegant,' replied Mary.

'Is it true that she was jilted at the altar?' inquired Daphne.

'Yeah. All set to get married. Everything arranged. She was

literally waiting at the altar standing beside the priest, the church pews full and the bride-groom didn't turn up,' said Mary.

'Like that character in Dickens,' replied Daphne.

'Miss Havisham, that's right. Her life stops after she's jilted,' said Mary.

'I saw the film on TV the other week… the clock stops in her dining room, the wedding banquet is still on the dining table, including the wedding cake and it is covered in cobwebs,' said Daphne.

'And a spider walks over the table,' replied Mary grimacing.

After a few minites Mrs Roberts entered the self-service area where Mary and Daphne worked. She purchased some alcohol so Mary had to authorise the purchase on the self-service machine. Mrs Roberts took a shine to Mary and always had a chat with her.

'Thank you my dear,' the exquisite manners of Mrs Roberts on display.

'That's alright,' replied Mary.

'Quiet in here today,' Mrs Roberts observed.

'Very quiet,' replied Mary.

'And have you found yourself a suitable young man to marry yet?' she inquired jokingly.

'Not yet,' said Mary, an embarrassed expression on her face. At that Mrs Roberts moved closer to Mary, adopting a confidential manner.

'You must always dangle a man,' Mrs Roberts declared.

'Dangle?' replied Mary, looking interested but puzzled.

'That's right.' Mrs Roberts was now warming up to a subject that clearly excited her passion. Suddenly the sinister smile came into full view. 'You make them fall in love with you, then you walk away. You break their heart!' ouch! better! Love it.

At this she collected her shopping and took her leave. Daphne came over to Mary.

'What did she say to you?' Daphne inquired.

'She talked about men… you must always dangle a man… then when he falls in love with you… you break his heart!' said Mary.

'Just like Miss Havisham!' declared Daphne.

***

Each month a small middle-aged man would shop at Talbot's. Casually dressed, small in stature he had watery eyes and sometimes spoke to Mary. He had a very distinctive nose, bulbous in form. He would approach the alcohol section furtively and fill his basket with bottles of brandy and whisky. Mary was returning from the staff canteen when she passed the alcohol section. He would sometimes talk to staff. The man smiled at Mary when he saw her and he approached her.

'A person in my shoes does not like the C word,' he said as if taking Mary in his confidence.

'The C word?' inquired Mary looking puzzled.

'Cirhosis… cirhosis of the liver, it's a killer. Over the weekend my cousin decided to give me a lecture on the subject. So when you see me heading for the alcohol section you should try to steer meaway from it… toward the fish counter or the bakery maybe.'

'Ok, I'll do that,' replied Mary. At the same time Mary couldn't help notice his basket full of bottles of alcohol.

'Today however I'm celebrating,' he declared.

'What are you celebrating?' inquired Mary.

'My unbirthday,' he said cryptically.

'Unbirthday?' said Mary looking puzzled.

'The three hundred and sixty-four days of the year that are not my birthday!' he delared much to Mary's amusement.

At that he and Mary walked the short distance to the till area.

A number of staffed tills had long queues except one that had a short queue.

'I know that man… he's an undertaker. I wouldn't stand behind an undertaker in a queue. It may change my odds of living a long life.'

At this he took his leave and joined another queue. Mary joined her friend Daphne in the self-service section.

'See the man in the queue there, the small bald middle-aged man with broad shoulders?' Mary inquired.

'Yeah,' said Daphne.

'Well the guy who's fond of alcohol wouldn't stand behind him in the queue beacuase that guy is an undertaker,' said Mary.

'Well some people are superstitious,' replied Daphne.

'That undertaker looks like a large beetle,' observed Mary.

'Since talking to that girl you've got insects on the brain,' replied Daphne.

'That's it… he looks like a deathwatch beetle!' declared Mary.

***

The following day Mary was passing the fish counter when she saw the girl who was fascinated by insects. The girls' mother was engrossed in conversation with another woman, who was her neighbour. Mary stopped and the girl smiled at her.

'Hello,' said Mary.

'Hello… do you want to see my insects? The girl replied. Mary laughed.

'You've got some insects?' inquired Mary. The girl removed a jar from a bag she was carrying.

'Look,' she said holding up the jar. 'Spiders and caterpillars… see.'

Inside the jar Mary could see a number of insects crawling around. The girl then returned the jar to her bag. She continued.

'I saw handbags over there.' She pointed to an area near the entrance. 'When I grow up I'm going to get a handbag… women have lots of little things in a handbag and I'm going to put my insects in it!' Mary laughed. 'If you go to Mayflower woods near the big Oak tree there are lots of ladybirds there.'

'Ok,' replied Mary.

'Last week I went to Mayflower woods with my friend… it's a secret.'

At that the girl's mother broke off her conversation with the woman she was talking to and called her: 'Veronica.' The girl waved goodbye to Mary and re-joined her mother. Mary went to the self-service section and re-joined her colleague Daphne.

'I saw the little girl again. This time she had a jar of insects with her. Strange girl There's something going on there.' She paused. 'I have got a day off tomorrow. So have you. Fancy a picnic?'

'A picnic?' replied Daphne.

'Yeah we could go to Mayflower woods,' said Mary.

'Why not. I's a chance to re-connect with nature… and study insects!' Both Mary and Daphne laughed.

***

The following day Mary and Daphne ventured out to Mayflower woods with their picnic box. A sunny day, when they arrived at the outskirts of Mayflower woods they were met with the sound of birdsong. As they moved into the woods the sound of birdsong was ubiquitous. They followed a curved path, passing gnarled tree branches. They saw a butterfly hovering over a hedge. Mary and Daphne stopped to study the butterfly.

'Is that the painted lady?' inquired Daphne.

'Could be… I'm not sure. Wow have you been researching

butterflies? replied Mary.

'Well I did google butterflies…' At that the butterfly flew off. 'And one colourful butterfly was the painted lady.'

They both looked at the butterfly fly off. They continued to follow the curving path, the leaves brushing past their bodies. They walked over a branch that blocked the curving path. At one point they heard the sound a twig breaking. The sound was some distance off. They saw the contours of a dark figure and both Mary and Daphne, instinctively, stood still.

'It's a deer. Keep still,' whispered Mary.

Two minutes later the deer was gone. Mary and Daphne looked at each other; a look of wonder suffused their faces.

'Wow. Awesome!' declared Daphne.

'Definiely awesome,' affirmed Mary. 'Let's find a spot where we have a picnic.'

'Ok,' replied Daphne.

They saw The Big Oak Tree and an arrow and headed for that. When they arrived at The Big OakTree they stopped and removed the food from their bag. They suddenly heard approaching footsteps; and from the undrgrowth and branches emerged a little girl. The same girl who shopped at Talbot's with her mother.

'Hello, you're the ladies from the supermarket,' said the girl recognising Mary and Daphne.

'Hello, it's Veronica isn't it? said Mary searching her memory.

'Are you on your own? inquired Daphne.

'Yes, I live next to the woods,' replied Veronica. Mary and Daphne looked concerned.

'We'll take you back to your home if you like,' said Mary.

'After I've collected some insects.' She held up a jar. 'Then I'll go home,' said Veronica.

Mary and Daphne looked at each other and shrugged their

shoulders. She continued.

'There are insects everywhere,' she said with unrestrained excitement. 'Look there's a spider's web,' she said pointing to a spider's web underneath the branch of a tree. 'Watch.' She unscrewed the jar and removed an ant from the jar and guided on to the spider's web. The ant struggled in the web as the spider davanced toward it. Then the spider overwhelmed the ant. 'Look its eating the ant.'

Mary and Daphne watched this grisly scene and grimaced at each other. Veronica watched the scene with intense interest. Then she turned to Mary.

'Have you got cobwebs between your legs?' she asked as if it was perfectly normal to ask such a question.

'No no!' said Mary, startled and shocked.

'Sit down we've got some spare sandwiches,' said Daphne. All three sat down and tucked into the sandwiches.

'So what's the fascination with insects?' inquired Mary.

'Well they're small and some are fat and some are skinny and they all have different shapes. Beetles are different from ladybirds.' She paused to eat her sandwich. 'Sometimes I talk to trees. Do trees know the alphabet? Veronica inquired.

'No,' replied Mary laughing.

'There's something in my shoe,' exclaimed Daphne with a look of alarm on her face. She took off her shoe and out ran a beetle.

'It's a beetle!'exclaimed Veronica, a look of joy splashed over her face. 'Do you put blood on your lips?'

'Blood?' Daphne looked perplexed. 'You mean lipstick. Yes I do,' replied Daphne.

'Mummy says that everyone has an angel looking over them and that angels live in heaven. Heaven is far away up there.' She points upward to the sky. 'Can you get there by aeroplane?' she inquired casually.

'I don't think so,' replied Mary baffled. She looked at Daphne.

'I don't like insects. When you go underground… when your as dead as a doornail… they eat you, they eat flesh. I once had a cat Napoleon. It died and we buried it in the garden. Later I dug up the ground but the insects had eaten him all up,' declared Veronica, to the evident surprise of Mary and Daphne.

'I tell you what, why don't we take you home to your mum,' said Mary becoming uneasy about the turn in the conversation. Daphne looked at Mary clearly in agreement.

'Stephen stole my watch!' exclaimed Veronica suddenly.

'Who's Stephen?' inquired Mary.

'My friend. I was collecting insects. First he said I was ugly then he stole my watch. I pushed him and he baged his head on the ground. There was blood from his head and he didn't move. It was an accident.' Mary and Daphne exchanged horrified glances.

Veronica walked over to an area to the right of a large tree, behind a tangle of brushes and branches. There was a small piece of level ground that was broken by a small mound of soil and leaves. Mary and Daphne followed Veronica. She knelt down beside this sall mound of earth and looked at it vacatly. She moved some soil and there appeared a human hand. Next to it a caterpillar moved slowly. She picked up the caterpillar, Mary and Daphne stared at the hand in horror. The mystery of the missing boy was solved.

'The insects will eat Stephen just like they ate Napoleon,' Veronica said matter of factly.

Disturbing but brilliant + darkly
twist didn't see coming

We Are Family

'Who Is Dante?' blazed the headline in the Daily Mail. The newspaper reported a spate of suspicious fires in London, in a warehouse and a nightclub. The police had evidence that the fires were started deliberately. There was also evidence that the fires were the work of the same person. Interviews with persons of interest in each fire revealed that a person named Dante had been hired to carry out the fires. The name was obviously a pseudonym. But nobody was able to identify Dante or give a clear description of Dante. The only clue was that she was a young woman. A team had been assembled by the Metroplitan police to investigate the fires. A concerted effort was being made by the police to find the culprit. Dante's = Inferno = clever.

***

Hyacinth was at home in her flat and decided to text her twin sister with the news that she had just purchased a car.

Hyacinth: bought a new car. Hyacinth = Dante?

Deborah: Wow. What make?

Hyacinth: Silver Vauxhall Corsa.

Deborah immediately phoned her sister. Hyacinth had already outstripped her twin in that unlike her twin she had passed her driving test. Apart from a ripple of jealousy Deborah could not understand how her sister could afford a brand-new car. Hyacinth said she saved the money. But Deborah remained baffled.

***

Hyacinth accompanied her twin sister Deborah to the Art Gallery for the exhibition of David's new paintings. David was Deborah's boyfriend. They had been going out for two years.

Handsome, louche David had an abundance of self-confidence. Deborah had to twist Hyacinth's arm to come to the exhibition. She didn't really want to go because she loathed David. The art gallery was a dreamy white space dotted with paintings. The exhibition featured two of his paintings, both depicting the naked female form. David greeted the sisters and then moved to his paintings. The art gallery was full of people whose aesthetic sensibility was so honed that they were able to identify a work of art immediately.

'Well do you like them? he inquired.

'They're beautiful,' declared Deborah.

Hyacinth smiled and remained silent. She remained indifferent to the paintings, a fact that was not lost on David. Hyacinth found his arrogance repellent and his supercilious attitudes toward other people repellent. But for the sake of her sister, she had to bite her lip and exude warm politeness. The adage love is blind came to mind when she looked at her sister. Hyacinth knew that one day David would betray her sister.

***

Hyacinth, on her day off from working at Talbot's supermarket, had decided to take a walk in Greenwich Park. Being a sunny day, the park was thronged with people. Hyacinth always walked at a brisk pace; she was proud of her physical fitness. She was walking on a path that led upwards toward the Greenwich Observatory. In the distance she noted a couple walking in front of her. Nothing extraordinary about that. Except that the male half of this romantic couple seemed familiar. The couple held hands and at one point stopped and kissed. At one point the man turned around. He was tall and thin with an aquiline nose. Now Hyacinth was certain. She knew the man. It was David, her twin sister's boyfriend. The woman he had kissed was not Deborah.

***

Hyacinth and Deborah, identical twins, were sitting in the canteen of Talbot's supermarket drinking a coffee. Both were fiery and feisty, and their relationship moved from one extreme to another, like a pendulum. Sometimes it was sweet harmony, sometimes bitter acrimony.

'David showed me the portrait yesterday. It was beautiful,' gushed Deborah.

David was a man who despised social convention. He had been working on a portrait of Deborah for a while. Hyacinth was not impressed by his artistic talent. The first time she met him she had him down, not as a friend but a foe.

Hyacinth recalled being invited, along with her twin sister, to what he grandly called his gallery. This turned out to be the shed in his garden where he painted, kept the tools of his trade and kept his paintings. Hyacinth recollected one painting, a portrait of an old woman. It was a grotesque vision of decaying human flesh. Somehow David's paintings fetched large amounts of money.

'You've got stars in your eyes,' observed Hyacinth rather coldly.

'Have I?' said Deborah.

At that moment music floated across Talbot's supermarket. It was a song by Donna Summer called This Time I Know it's for Real.

'So this time it's for real?' inquired Hyacinth, prompted by the song.

'Maybe,' said Deborah coyly.

Should she tell her sister that she had seen David embracing another woman, kissing another woman?

'Did you see Star Trek last night, the episode The Menagerie?' inquired Hyacinth.

The twins were avid fans of the captivating science fiction series.

'Yes, I did,' said Deborah.

'The captain of the Star ship Enterprise encounters creatures that have the power to create illusions,' said Hyacinth. She stared at Deborah, then continued. 'You're relationship with David is an illusion. He doesn't love you. He's going to hurt you!'

'Whenever I'm happy, whenever I'm in love you just can't take it. Can you?' Deborah said this with unrestrained fury. She stood up from the table and stalked off. Hyacinth watched her walk off.

***

'I've found a place to live, I got it the hard way.

A permanent address to give,

I got it for always.

Nobody can tear me loose.

They tell me there's no escape.

On Heartache Avenue.'

The lyrics to the song floated around Benny's bar on Ocean pier. The bar was dimly lit, wall lights shining brightly, dotted around the room. The bar was half full, various people engaged in conversation. Hyacinth and Trevor were sitting at a table, smiling and staring at each other. Hearing the song Hyacinth's eyes lit up.

'That's my mum's favourite song,' she declared.

'Sorry, what's it called?' said Trevor with some embarrassment.

'Heartache Avenue by the Maisonettes,' said Hyacinth.

'It's a nice song,' said Trevor.

'It's a beautiful song.' There was a pause. 'I want to see you again Trevor.'

'I want to see you again Hyacinth.'

Then they kissed.

***

Ocean pier occupied a special place in the hearts of the twins.

A quintessential pleasure pier it evoked family memories. Hyacinth always thought that the pier reminded her of a huge hand extending out to sea. Their beloved mother took them to the pier when they were children. Assailed by the sights and sounds of the amusement arcade they were mesmerised by the pinball machines and the game Pac-man. Much to Hyacinth's annoyance Deborah was more adept at the game.

Constructed during the Victorian era iron pillars supported a wooden structure. It had amused soldiers on leave during the second world war. It had amused star-struck lovers. It had amused pensioners dozing on deckchairs. It had amused wild-eyed, energetic children.

The amusement arcade, Benny's bar, a carousal, the card shop and the confectionery store all formed a part of the rich tapestry of the pier. Hyacinth and Deborah sometimes wandered under the pier, throwing pebbles into the sea, dwarfed by the massive structure. Walking on the pier Deborah liked to peer through the gaps in the wood at the sea below. Unlike her twin Deborah was fascinated by water.

Hyacinth had her first kiss on Ocean pier. As did Deborah. Hyacinth fell in love on the pier as did her twin sister. When their mother was swallowed up by eternity the twins took refuge at the pier. They both got drunk then peered out to sea, longing for their mother.

Later, walking on the pier Deborah stopped and turned to Hyacinth, dramatically and said,' One day I'm getting married on this pier!'

***

Hyacinth's earliest memory of Ocean Pier was of the Vintage Amusement Arcade. Stepping inside was like stepping out of one century and stepping into another century. The curator of this cabinet of curiosities was an elderly man called Mark whose sorrowful face belied a friendly soul. He looked after the arcade in the same way that an ageing priest looked after his small church.

As you entered the arcade, he occupied a small booth. Sometimes his dog Elsa lay snoozing next to the booth, as was the case on this day. The arcade contained objects and artefacts from another age. What the Butler Saw, the Laughing Sailor, various penny arcade games contained in oak panelled frames adhered to the wall.

There were various photographs on the wall of old actors famous for playing Dracula, including Bela Lugosi. He had once visited the pier and signed a photograph many decades ago when Mark's father ran The Vintage Amusement Arcade. Until told by Mark the twins had never heard of him.

The Laughing Sailor laughed with manic intensity, the laughter emanating from a scary plastic face. The twins investigated the viewfinder of What the Butler Saw, laughing and sniggering to themselves. A beautiful woman was lounging on a long settee. A man entered, then the film ended.

But what sent shivers down the spines of the twins was the clown displayed in a showcase. He had an other-worldly smile. Hyacinth was mesmerised, checking his eyes and his mouth, fixated on the eerie clown.

'I'm sure I saw its eyes move!' declared Hyacinth.

'Come on! Let's go!' railed Deborah.

When they reached the exit Mark, the curator stepped out of his booth. He had a serious expression on his face.

'Listen girls. There's somebody working on this pier who is very dangerous. Be careful!

The twins looked perplexed and then took their leave. The following week the twins visited the pier. Strolling along the pier they encountered Mark. The daylight was fading and above the pier seagulls were emitting a mournful cry. Seeing the twins, he stopped and looked upward into the darkness. He had a strange look in his eyes.

'Listen to the children of the night. What music they make!' he declared.

Mark is eccentric or just mad?

He then took his leave. The twins recognised this as a quote from the film Dracula. This was exactly the sort of thing the twins expected Mark to say. This was the last time they saw Mark and the Vintage Amusement Arcade. The next time they visited the pier it was replaced by a more modern arcade with a raft of noisy, gaudy video games. But Hyacinth remembered Mark's warning.

***

Hyacinth recalled her mother's love of old films. One afternoon their mother watched an old film called Whatever Happened to Baby Jane. The twins watched the film along with their mother. The film involved two of Beryl's favourite actresses, Bette Davis and Joan Crawford. Bette Davis, caked in make-up and wearing children's clothes, looked particularly grotesque. At the same time Hyacinth was drawn by Davis's ferocity and intensity.

The twins watched this excursion into gothic melodrama with total fascination. The story focuses on two ageing actresses. The sisters move to an old mansion after Blanche, played by Joan Crawford, is disabled in a car accident and is confined to a wheelchair. Jane, played by Bette Davis, becomes Blanche's carer. But the relationship is poisoned by mutual hatred. The narrative hints that Jane was driving the car that caused Blanche's injuries.

In one scene Jane presents Blanche with her evening meal. The meal is presented on a tray. When Blanche lifts the silver lid off the plate, she is faced with a plate containing a dead rat!

Beryl, Deborah and Hyacinth all gasped in horror when they saw this scene.

'When we get old and if we lived together you'd never do that to me would you Deborah?'

'Of course not Hyacinth. We are family,' said Deborah.

***

On their eleventh birthday Hyacinth and Deborah were taken to Ocean pier by their beloved mother Beryl. Beryl, whose elfin beauty and sweet smile she had passed on to the twins, had organised a treasure hunt for the twins. The task set was to find four envelopes, the final envelope containing money for the twins. The four envelopes could be found anywhere on the pier, including in shops. In advance Beryl had talked to various retailers and people on the pier and handed over the envelopes.

Beryl sat down on the deckchair, drinking in the sea view off the pier.

'Remember there are four envelopes. The first clue is that you need these two things for sandcastles. Good luck!'

'Ok mum,' said Deborah.

Hyacinth and Deborah glanced at each other, full of energy and excitement. They walked swiftly around the pier.

'Let's look at the souvenir shop!' declared Hyacinth.

The woman behind the counter smiled at the twins when they entered the souvenir shop. They looked at the postcards, the various bric a brac and then suddenly Deborah saw the bucket and spade.

'That's what you need to build a sandcastle!' said Hyacinth.

Hyacinth picked up the bucket and spade and handed them over, with some money, to the woman behind the counter. She completed the financial transaction and then produced an envelope from under the counter.

'Your Hyacinth and Deborah aren't you. Your mum asked me to give you this envelope.'

Hyacinth thanked the woman and then opened the envelope. A piece of paper in the envelope contained the following message: they are colourful, and some people are afraid of them.

'People are afraid of them? repeated Hyacinth.

They went in and out of shops on the pier. Then Deborah saw the clown juggling.

'People have a fear of clowns' don't they? declared Deborah.

Confused where this is going? How is this relevant to the fires?

'And they're colourful! said Hyacinth.

They rushed over to him. The clown stopped juggling.

'Ah! The twins. Deborah and Hyacinth. 'He put his hand in his pocket. 'Your mother told me that you'll be looking for this. 'He handed over the envelope.

Deborah opened the envelope and she read out the following message.

'I am not square shaped or triangular. I keep on moving. Children like me.'

'Children like me?' said Hyacinth.

Hyacinth and Deborah looked around the pier. They looked puzzled. Then Deborah saw the merry go round.

'Got it,' said Deborah.

She pointed at the merry go round. There were a couple of children on the carousal. They both approached the carousal and the female assistant smiled as they approached.

'You're the twins, Deborah and Hyacinth?' she said.

'That's right,' said Hyacinth.

'You want this.'

The young woman pulled out an envelope and handed it over to Hyacinth.

'Thanks,' said Hyacinth.

Hyacinth opened the envelope and read the message inside.

'I'm soft and cold. I taste nice on a summer's day.'

'I'm soft and cold?' repeated Deborah.

'And I taste nice on a summer's day…?' repeated Hyacinth. She looked around the pier. Then she smiled. 'We've got this licked! Ice cream!'

Positioned at the front of the pier was an ice cream booth. A tall thin young man served ice cream in the booth. He smiled as the twins approached.

'So tell me who's Deborah and who's Hyacinth?' he inquired.

'I'm Hyacinth and this is Deborah,' said Hyacinth pointing to her sister.

He stared at the twins for a period that was disconcerting.

'So Hyacinth has got green eyes and Deborah has got blue eyes!' he said with a note of triumph.

All three laughed at this observation. He pulled out an envelope from his pocket. He continued.

'You'll be wanting this.'

He handed the envelope over to Deborah.

'Thanks.'

Both twins were delighted that they had completed the treasure hunt. They opened the envelope and divided the money between them. But for Hyacinth the triumph was tempered by the palpable unease she felt in the presence of the ice cream vendor. His eyes were cold but unlike the ice cream he sold they had no soft quality.

***

The twins were transfixed by the arrival of the fire eater on Ocean Pier. A crowd gathered around him as he prepared to start his act. Their mother was having a nap on the deckchair, that faced out to sea. A small thin man, the fire eater seemed lost in concentration.

'Ladies and gentlemen, the following act is dangerous. Do not copy this act!' he declared.

His act consisted of two parts. The first was fire eating. He held a torch in his right hand, a piece of cloth attached to the end of the torch. He lighted the torch and then placed the torch in his mouth, instantly extinguishing the flame. The crowd gasped, including Deborah and Hyacinth. The second part was fire breathing. He lit the torch again. He picked up a small bottle from the ground and took a swig of the contents. He then spat out the liquid through the flame, creating a plume of flame. This was a feast to the eyes. Everyone applauded, including the twins. The image of the the plume of flame stayed in Hyacinth's mind long after the fire eater departed.

***

Hyacinth stared at the dripping clock above the front door of Benny's bar on Ocean pier. She Deborah and their mother were sitting at a table on the concourse of the pier sipping drinks. The upper half of the clock was oval shaped. The lower half of the clock tapered inward so that the numbers five, six and seven were elongated. Hyacinth had always been fascinated by the clock.

'Why is that clock shaped like that mummy?' asked Hyacinth.

'That's the dripping clock. It's based on a famous painting by a famous painter called…?' Beryl struggled to remember the name of the painter. 'Salvador… Salvador Dali. That's it!'

'What does it mean, a dripping clock?' asked Hyacinth.

Beryl looked puzzled.

'I'm not sure. Something about time and memory I think,' she said.

'So time is dripping away!' declared Hyacinth.

Beryl and Deborah smiled.

'Yeah that's right love. Time is dripping away!' agreed Beryl.

Hyacinth continued to stare at the clock mesmerised.

***

One evening the twins and their mother attended the karaoke night at Benny's bar. That night created an image of Beryl forever locked in the memories of the twins. Benny's bar was swarming with people, the air thick with the hum of conversation. First the twins gave their rendition of the pop hit Showing Out by Mel and Kim.

They were word perfect, and their dance moves perfectly choreographed in time with the music. Their performance was met with rapturous applause. Hyacinth and Deborah returned to their table smiling and jubilant. Beryl kissed them both.

Beryl and her friend, Marjorie, who both shared an effervescent smile, decided to give a rendition of the song Yes Sir I can Boogie by Baccara. The twins looked at each other with dismay. They recalled seeing the song on TV and it was deeply uncool. As Beryl and Marjorie approached the stage the twins cringed expecting a hugely embarrassing experience. But when they started to sing a hush descended on the audience. They danced in slow rhythm to the music.

'Mister your eyes are full of hesitation

Sure, makes me wonder

If you know what you are looking for

Um baby I want to keep my reputation

I'm a sensation

You try me once you'll beg for more

Ooh yes sir I can boogie…'

Deborah and Hyacinth watched transfixed. Their mother and Marjorie gave an enchanting performance. Beryl looked beautiful and she delivered the lyrics with a fine singing voice that enraptured the audience.

***

Florence's' tattoo parlour was quiet, the walls adorned with images of a variety of animals. Snakes, dragons, wolves, butterflies, scorpions, lions, tigers, cats, bats and eagles they all assailed the eye. Florence had known the twins for several years. About the same age they chatted about this and that and sometimes about their romantic entanglements.

'So what's the job today?' inquired Florence.

'I want you to give me a tattoo of a heart and next to it the words I Love Trevor!' said Hyacinth.

'No problem. Well, somebody is loved up. Trevor… a strong masculine name,' observed Florence. 'And how's Deborah?

'Well… she's going through a rough patch now. Love trouble,' said Hyacinth.

'Ah. Well, you know what my mother used to say. When the sun sets on one romance, the sun rises on another,' said Florence.

They both laughed.

***

Hyacinth and Deborah lived in separate flats in south London, three miles apart. Hyacinth was sitting at home watching television when she received a text from her sister.

Deborah: me and David have split up.

Hyacinth: sorry to hear that.

Deborah: he is seeing someone else. Our relationship is dead in the water.

Hyacinth was tempted to ring her sister but given the bruising conversation they had the day before and the bad news Deborah had just received she decided not to.

***

Hyacinth and Deborah were on their break, drinking coffee in the staff canteen at Talbot's. Deborah was looking downcast; Hyacinth noted that her make-up had not been applied properly.

'You're going to say I told you so aren't you! declared Deborah bitterly.

'No, I'm not,' said Hyacinth.

They sat in silence for a few minutes, Deborah fidgeting anxiously.

'Did you see the local news?' Deborah asked.

'No,' said Hyacinth.

'A fire was reported on a property in north London. A shed was burnt down. The night of the fire there was thunder and lightning, so the police think the shed was probably hit by a bolt of lightning. 'said Deborah.

'No way!' exclaimed Hyacinth. Hyacinth stared at her sister. 'It wasn't David's shed?'

'The owner of the shed was a painter. Most of his paintings were kept in the main house but two were stored in the shed. These were destroyed, according to the news report. It was David's shed! said Deborah.

'Well every cloud has a silver lining!' said Hyacinth and the two sisters' laughed.

***

The low murmur of voices rising from each table created a quiet symphony of sound in the restaurant. Hyacinth had decided to invite her sister to join her for a meal out with her beau (that's what she called her boyfriend, her beau). Trevor was handsome, loud and brash. A businessman he dressed sharply and at work was not averse to sharp practice.

The restaurant was full. Trevor lifted his glass.

'To the heavenly sisters!'

Deborah and Hyacinth lifted their glasses and they all joined in the ritual of clinking their glasses together. Hyacinth was intoxicated in Trevor's presence and the intoxication had nothing to do with alcohol. Although her mood was despondent Deborah decided to try, to engage in conversation.

'How's work Trevor?' inquired Deborah.

'Just cleared a lucrative property deal. I'm riding the crest of a wave' he replied with his usual expansive confidence.

'Your summertime sadness won't last,' declared Hyacinth to

Deborah.

This was a reference to the song summertime sadness by Lana Del Rey, a song that both sisters liked.

'There's plenty more fish in the sea!' declared Trevor with brash optimism.

'I've got my red dress on tonight, dancing in the dark, in the pale moonlight…' sang Hyacinth.

'Done my hair up real big, beauty queen style, high heels off, I'm feeling alive!' sang Deborah, completing the song lyrics.

All three laughed heartily.

***

Do twin sisters' have secrets from each other? Yes, they do. At the restaurant Hyacinth thought she noticed something going on between Deborah and Trevor. Glances between the two; a frisson between the two maybe? Then she discarded the thought. After all they were sisters. As for Hyacinth herself she pursued her own shadow life and held her own dark secret that her twin was totally unaware of.

Alone in her flat, the rain was beating against the windowpane when Hyacinth received the text. She stared at the text, baffled. The text read: I love you, Deborah. Then she stared at the name at the end of the text. The name stood out; it was Trevor. She tried to work out what had just happened. Hyacinth had received a text, meant for her sister, that had been sent to her by mistake from her boyfriend Trevor. Trevor was in love with her twin sister. She felt queasy; the earth cut from under her feet.

She phoned Trevor; the call went straight to voicemail. She texted a message to call her. She did the same with her twin sister; again, her call went straight to voicemail. Both avoided her calls and messages.

The next day Hyacinth received a text from Trevor. It was succinct: I'm sorry. Trevor eventually answered his phone.

'Well?' inquired Hyacinth.

'I'm sorry,' Trevor replied quietly.

'So we're finished!' Hyacinth paused. 'That's it. And with my sister!' she exclaimed.

'Look…'he replied, but Hyacinth interrupted him.

'You bastard!' she exclaimed and ended the call.

***

Hyacinth tried continuously to phone her sister, but she did not answer her phone. She thought about going round to her flat in person, but she knew that if she did this, she would not only lose her self-control but also her dignity. Deborah eventually answered the phone.

'So it's true?' Hyacinth inquired forcefully.

'Yes,' Deborah replied timidly.

'How could you. You are my sister?' Hyacinth's voice was drenched in emotion.

'Things happen!' Deborah said coldly.

At this Hyacinth ended the phone call. A double betrayal intensified the pain. Despite clinging to life Hyacinth decided there and then to exact revenge. Her twin sister had no idea of her shadow life; of what she was capable of.

***

'My sister has plunged a dagger into my heart! She is a traitor!'

Mary, plump and affable was in the canteen at Talbot's supermarket listening to Hyacinth, one of her colleagues who worked in the warehouse. Hyacinth had elfin features and beautiful almond eyes. She came into this world shortly before her twin, Deborah. To be exact five minutes and ten seconds before her twin sister. Deborah was punctual whereas Hyacinth tended to be late; Deborah loved animals whereas Hyacinth did not; and Hyacinth tended to be more ill-tempered. But both sisters could be devious when it suited their purposes. Now there was a rip in the universe; they were at total loggerheads.

'My sister has fallen on love with my boyfriend!'

'Oh,' exclaimed Mary. She did not know how to respond to this revelation.

'My own sister… what a bitch!' continued Hyacinth. 'Anyhow I've got to go.' Hyacinth took her leave, clearly agitated.

Mary was joined at the table by her friend Daphne. Physically they were a study in contrasts; Mary small and plump, Daphne taller, adopting a Goth look. They were both sweet natured, who bounced oddball ideas off each other as naturally as night followed day. Their mundane jobs did not restrict their imaginations. Presently their imaginations were fired by a film they saw on television called Calamity Jane, played by Doris Day, based on the life of an American frontierswoman in the nineteenth century. Their conversation was peppered with quotes from the film.

'Hi. what's up?'

'I've just been talking to Hyacinth. She's had a major falling out with her sister. She said that Deborah has stolen her boyfriend…'

'Wow,' exclaimed Daphne.

'You know what happens when two sticks of dynamite rub up against each other… an explosion!'

'The deadwood stage is rolling on over the plains,' said Daphne.

***

Henry, tall and whippet thin, worked as an assistant manager at Talbot's. He liked to tease Mary and Daphne with questions about the meaning of obscure words and the answers to riddles. Mary was working on the self-service tills; she saw him approaching her.

'What can you catch but can't throw?' inquired Mary.

'A cold,' he answered triumphantly. Mary was crestfallen. He continued with another question. 'What's the difference between an aesthete and an anaesthetist?'

Mary paused and gathered her thoughts. Then she smiled.

'Well an aesthete tries to knock you out with the beauty of art whereas an anaesthetist tries to knock you out with drugs!'

Mary was triumphant; Henry turned and walked off briskly. The self -service tills became quite busy. A couple nearby began to quarrel whilst operating the self-service till. A man, a regular of Talbot's supermarket, asked Mary for some assistance. Small and smartly dressed Mary often conversed with him and he told her once that he was an actor. Unsurprisingly, he had a clear, resonant voice. He looked at the quarrelling couple and remarked.

'The course of true love never did run smooth.'

'A Midsummer Night's Dream,' she replied promptly.

'Young lady… you have an appreciation of art. Wonderful!' He took his shopping and walked away.

Daphne looked at Mary, surprised and impressed, in equal measure.

'You know when I was at school, I never liked Shakespeare.'

'Why? inquired Mary.

'Well… Hamlet, King Lear and all those stories all had one thing in common.'

'What was that?'

'No car chases!'

***

At secondary school the twins tended to be hyperactive and disruptive, their brains bored with wordy teaching lessons. But one science lesson captured Hyacinth's attention. Despite being distracted by the gangly, goofy physical appearance of the teacher the lesson turned out to be compelling.

'The ancient Greeks said that everything in the universe is made of four elements. Can you tell me what those four elements are?'

There were about twenty pupils in the class and several hands shot up.

'Water!' declared Deborah.

'Good Deborah!' said the teacher.

'Air!' declared another pupil.

'Excellent Nigel!

'Earth!' declared the pupil at the back of the class.'

Hyacinth's eyes blazed with triumph. Clearly, she knew the fourth element.

'Fire!' declared Hyacinth.

***

George was at his wits end. Small and wiry he was exhausted by anxiety. He was in the White Horse drinking a pint of beer. The White Horse was a small pub with a feel of intimacy. He was sitting at a table when he was joined by his friend Eric, a picture of exuberant optimism.

'What did the publican say to Shakespeare when he walked in the pub?' Eric said with a large smile on his face.

'I don't know,' said George warily.

'You're barred!' Eric declared, delighted with the punchline. 'Shakespeare… the bard?'

But George did not laugh. Eric probed further.

'What's the matter mate?'

'It's the restaurant. I'm bedevilled by problems. Takings are down, customer numbers are down, I owe money to the bank. If things don't improve the business will fold,' George replied with wary resignation.

'There's somebody that may be able to help you,' Eric said. Suddenly, he looked shifty, looking to his left and right. 'Have you heard of Dante?'

'Dante? No,' George replied.

'Dante fixes problems. Dante can help you trust me,' said Eric decisively.

'How?' inquired George.

'A desperate situation requires a desperate remedy. Dante can only be contacted on the dark web. Shall I try to fix you up with a meeting?'

'This remedy… is it legal? inquired George.

'Shall I arrange a meeting, yes, or no?' asked Eric.

'Go ahead,' said George diving into the unknown.

***

George eventually located the abandoned warehouse on the edge of a soulless industrial estate. A wire fence circled the warehouse. George looked for an entry point and soon found a gap where the wire fence had collapsed. He found a side door and entered the warehouse, a vast and dilapidated area. It was silent, cold and eerie. The agreed time for the meeting was seven pm; it was now a few minutes before the hour. Suddenly he heard footsteps. Then he saw a small figure come through the door he had used. The small figure wore dark clothes and had a face mask. The figure stopped when it saw George.

'Dante?' inquired George nervously.

'I'm Dante,' said the figure in an unmistakably female voice. 'You need help with a problem?'

'My restaurant,' said George.

'You want somebody to torch your restaurant?' said the woman.

'Yes,' said George.

'That will cost fifteen thousand pounds,' the woman said curtly.

'I'll need a few days to get the money,' said George shaken by the price tag of the job.

'How many floors?' Inquired the woman.

'Two floors. The flat above the restaurant is empty now. It is being renovated,' said George.

'Good. The property must be empty when I torch it,' said the woman.

'We close at ten o'clock. After that the property is empty,' said George.

'Any CCTV?' the woman inquired.

'No,' replied George.

'Once you give me the money I'll do the job,' declared the woman.

'I'll get it for you in three days,' said George.

'We'll meet here on Friday, same time,' said the woman.

'OK,' said George. He handed her a piece of paper. 'Here's the name and address of the restaurant.'

Dante took the piece of paper. Then the mysterious, masked figure took her leave.

***

In 1977 a bolt of lightning hit an electricity substation on the Hudson River. This caused a massive blackout in New York city. The blackout sparked civil disorder and several arson attacks on buildings. Dante recalled this fact after reading an article about the blackout. Darkness is a natural ally of the criminal. An area of London, encompassing the location of the restaurant, had just been plunged into darkness due to a power cut. She had received her payment; therefore, she decided to re-schedule the arson attack on the restaurant, to take advantage of the power cut. She decided to launch the attack immediately.

***

A group of staff were sitting in Talbot's canteen sipping coffee and shooting the breeze including Mary, Daphne, and Hyacinth. The focus of conversation was a news report in the newspapers.

'So who is Dante?' inquired Daphne, posing the question to everyone at the table.

'Abandon hope all ye who enter here!' declared Henry cryptically. Everyone at the table could not understand the reference.

'What does that mean Henry?' inquired Mary.

'Dante was an Italian writer… that was the inscription on the gates of hell when he arrived at the gates of hell. He wrote a poem called the Divine Comedy. The first part of it was called Inferno and was about his journey through hell. 'Henry liked to display his learning to everyone.

'I'm talking about the news report about the arson attack on the restaurant in London. The man charged with the attack said that he didn't carry out the attack, it was carried out by a woman called Dante,' declared Daphne irritated by Henry's interjection.

'Statistically arsonists are more likely to be men than women aren't they?' asserted Mary.

'Definitely!' said Henry.

'It's the power and the glory… that's why arsonists do it. The power and the glory,' opined Hyacinth very quietly. Everybody on the table looked at her.

'Brilliant observation Hyacinth,' declared Henry.

'I'm going on a fire safety course next Wednesday and I was reading up on arsonists,' said Hyacinth.

Mary and Daphne stared at Hyacinth, and both thought about

her rage at her twin sister Deborah.

***

Mary, Henry and Daphne, on hearing the fire alarm, began to instruct customers to leave the store and assemble outside. People hesitated and were not quite sure what to do and had to be told by staff to leave the building. After a couple of minutes, the store was vacated. The fire brigade arrived and entered the building. After about fifteen minutes the fire brigade left the store, and everybody could re-enter the store.

Apparently, a wastepaper bin in the warehouse caught fire and triggered the fire alarm. It was a small fire and once the alarm was raised it was dealt with by the fire brigade. The fire was started by a discarded cigarette that set some paper alight in the wastepaper bin. The manager Mr Henderson talked to staff on duty, but was unable to identify the person who discarded the cigarette. It was classed as an accidental fire. Mary and Daphne were in the canteen drinking coffee.

'You don't think it was started, deliberately, do you?' Daphne said nervously, looking around her.

'An arsonist working here! Impossible!' proclaimed Mary.

***

The fire safety course was held in a grey building full of nondescript rooms. There were about fifteen people in attendance. But the course instructor and course participants were totally unaware of one extraordinary fact: one of the participants was an arsonist. That person of course was Hyacinth. She attended the course with eager anticipation. Ironically the paraphernalia of fire prevention fascinated her.

The course covered the different types of fire, from materials such as wood, from electrical equipment, from gases and from flammable liquids such as petrol. This was Hyacinth's preferred method of ignition. The course instructor gave some statistics on the number of fires caused by cigarettes. He also covered the fire triangle; the three requirements for every fire. These were oxygen, heat and fuel. The fire triangle was Hyacinth's idea of heaven.

The highlight of the course for Hyacinth was the video on a real-life fire and how people reacted to the fire. The video focused on a fire in a hotel. The video was notable for two reasons: first, the people in the hotel were slow to react and second the speed at which the fire gathered pace was startling. Whilst everyone attending the course watched the video with grave concern Hyacinth could barely contain her excitement.

Hyacinth regarded firefighters as uniformed killjoys. She recalled an image of firefighters arriving at her school when she was a teenager because someone in the school had activated the fire alarm system as a hoax. The headmaster described such people as the lunatic fringe. Hyacinth used to climb on the window ledge in the toilets and light a match under the smoke alarm. She was the lunatic fringe!

During the afternoon her mind drifted to a film she had seen recently called Once Upon a Time in Hollywood. Hyacinth recalled a scene where a soldier during the second world war dispatches some of the enemy with a flame thrower. She would love to purchase a flame thrower, but this of course was prohibited by an act of Parliament.

Later, in the course, the instructor spoke about arson and gave some alarming statistics on arson in the United Kingdom. During the period 2012 to 2013 there were 23,700 deliberate fires recorded in the United Kingdom. Forty-five per cent of deliberate fires occurred in road vehicles. Hyacinth reflected that, hitherto, she had never engaged in this practice. Fifty-three per cent of deliberate fires occurred in buildings that were not dwellings. Of these nearly a third occurred in private garages, garden sheds, green houses or summer houses. Hyacinth listened to his talk with wry amusement. She was unable to share with the group her personal contribution to these statistics. She remembered the satisfaction she derived from torching Deborah's old boyfriends' garden shed. The group discussed the recent spate of fires in London and the identity of the culprit, a mysterious person called Dante.

'Dante should be put in prison for a hundred years!' declared Hyacinth.

***

Hyacinth stood on the fringe of the stockroom. Breaking a cardinal rule of fire prevention, she lit a cigarette. At that moment a manager saw that she was smoking and approached her. At the same time Hyacinth's twin sister appeared in the stockroom.

'You'll have to put out that cigarette,' the manager instructed Hyacinth. Deborah suddenly appeared next to her sister and glared at the manager.

'Do you really want to push this point?' Deborah asked her defiantly.

The manager looked at Deborah, then at Hyacinth. She then walked off. Deborah and Hyacinth looked at each other and did not say anything. Then Deborah walked off. The twins may be at loggerheads but when either one of them was threatened by the outside world they presented a united front.

***

Hyacinth recalled the incident at Ocean pier many years earlier when she was a teenager. Jugglers throwing clubs in the air, in perfect time and rhythm, clowns grimacing, the pier was vibrant with human life. The twins were wandering around the pier soaking up the atmosphere.

Hyacinth told Deborah she was going to the rest room. She entered the public toilet; it was empty and quiet. Suddenly she was aware somebody was behind her. In a second, she was grabbed from behind in a vice like grip. A hand was clasped around her mouth. The other hand fondled her breasts and probed between her legs. She was paralysed by fear. She could not move.

'Don't move. I'm not going to hurt you,' the man said in a menacing voice.

The man thrust himself up against her rear end. The whole thing lasted about three to four minutes.

'Don't shout!' he commanded.

The man removed his hand and then vanished. Hyacinth noted that he had a ring on the index finger of his right hand. She turned around and the toilet was empty. She wanted to cry but composed herself.

When she re-joined her sister, Deborah sensed something was wrong.

'What's the matter?'

'Somebody grabbed and groped me in the toilet!'

'What?' Are you ok? Did he hurt you?

'No! I'm fine.'

'We need to call the police!'

'No!' I'm fine.'

'But…'

'Forget it. I'm fine.'

'Did he?'

'No. He groped me nothing more.'

Hyacinth was insistent that she did not want to report the incident to the police.

The following week the twins revisited the pier. Sauntering along the pier Deborah decided to buy ice cream from the ice cream booth. The ice cream vendor smiled at Hyacinth. The twins knew the ice cream vendor as he was the same vendor who took part in the treasure hunt on their eleventh birthday a decade earlier and handed them the envelope with the money in it. A tall middle-aged man his eyes scanned her face. Hyacinth, standing nearby, watched the man flirt with her sister. But when he spoke Hyacinth recognised the voice instantly. When he handed the change to Deborah, she also noticed he had a ring on the index finger of his right hand. Now she was certain. Although she didn't see the man's face this was the man who attacked her. She decided not to share her suspicions with her sister.

A few days later Hyacinth returned to the pier alone. She had one thing on her mind. To find out where the ice cream vendor lived. She watched him from a discreet distance. He closed his ice cream booth at four o'clock each afternoon. She followed him as he weaved his way through the streets of the seaside town, past an array of souvenir shops and amusement arcades. He walked with a forceful stride. After twenty-five minutes he came to a caravan site. The site contained many caravans. He weaved his way through the caravans until he came to a caravan on the edge of the site. A small caravan painted white, it was grubby and rather sad looking. He pulled a key from his pocket and opened the caravan door. Now Hyacinth knew where he lived.

An hour later Hyacinth returned to the camp site. She identified her escape route, through the fence on the edge of the camp and then through the forest. The camp site was devoid of people walking around. Armed with a can of petrol and a bag containing branches and twigs she went to work. She placed a pile of tree branches and twigs at each end of the caravan and doused them with petrol. She struck a match setting fire to both piles of wood. She made a run for the fence, jumped over it and headed for the forest. She looked back and saw flames forming around the caravan.

Although asleep at the time the ice cream vendor woke up in time and managed to escape the fire. The caravan, engulfed in flames, was destroyed. The ice cream vendor survived, suffering from the effects of smoke inhalation. Despite a police investigation the arsonist was never identified or brought to justice.

***

Every year the younger staff at Talbot's held a retro disco. The disco was organised by Mary and Daphne. They were both sitting in the café of Talbot's supermarket drinking coffee when they were joined by Felicia, an ebullient cheerful Jamaican.

'Hi,' said Felicia.

'Hi,' said Mary.

'Hi Felicia. Wow you've lost some weight!' declared Daphne.

Whereupon Felicia produced her smartphone and displayed an image of herself to Mary and Daphne.

'The old me. And you see before you the new me. I've lost two stone!' she declared with triumph.

'Incredible!' declared Daphne. 'You're coming to the disco?'

'Sure. The twins and I will get everybody dancing,' said Felicia.

A hall was hired. Mary and Daphne obtained a disco ball. The ball consisted of shards of glass. The ball revolved from the ceiling and as it spun around it threw off small glints of light around the area below. Mary and Daphne also obtained large electric letters spelling out the words Retro Disco. These electric letters were applied to the wall at one end of the hall. Mary and Daphne both loved the joy and ecstasy of dancing. That sublime interplay between bodily movement and the thumping heartbeat of music on the dancefloor turned all anxieties and sad thoughts to pulp. They hired a disc jockey.

On the night of the disco the atmosphere in the hall gathered energy. Mary, Daphne, Hyacinth, Deborah amongst others attended. There was a crowd of about thirty. Alcoholic and soft drinks were served. Hyacinth and Deborah came separately. Identical twins they were small, lithe and beautiful. They moved in the same way, their bodies in harmony to the same swaying motion. They eyed each other warily, not acknowledging each other.

When Felicia saw Hyacinth, she approached and said that she Deborah and Hyacinth would set the dancefloor on fire. When Hyacinth saw her twin enter the hall, she really did want to set the dancefloor on fire.

The disc jockey played dance music from the seventies and eighties. The music flowed: Give It to Me Baby by Rick James, You're the One for Me by D Train, Don't Stop Til You Get Enough by Michael Jackson. The disco ball above threw off tiny rectangles of light that spun around the room.

Hyacinth danced in perfect harmony to the music, her limbs moving easily, her dancing hypnotic. Deborah also proved to be a hypnotic dancer. The music and dancing continued. Hyacinth blew Deborah a kiss; there was always a competition between the two. But this competition had a lethal edge.

Mary and Daphne also danced with joyful abandon. At the end of the evening, when the music stopped, the flickering lights from the disco ball had disappeared and the manic energy had subsided, Hyacinth approached Deborah.

'You broke the rules!' exclaimed Hyacinth.

'What rules?' said Deborah.

'What are the three components of the fire triangle?' inquired Hyacinth.

'What?' said a bewildered Deborah.

'You know all about triangles. I mean me and you are part of a triangle. So, let me tell you that the three components of the fire triangle are fuel, heat and oxygen. You're not as smart as you think you are. And my position on the triangle, well there's plenty of oxygen but no fuel or heat. You and David have a perfect fire triangle, plenty of heat and fuel there!' She paused and stared at her sister. 'Remember Deborah, we are family!'

'That's right… we are family.'

***

Mary and Daphne were in Talbot's canteen when they were joined by one of the twins.

'Wow Hyacinth! You can dance.' The twin paused, looked at Mary and Daphne, then smiled.

'Thanks.'

'How's things with Deborah?' inquired Daphne. There was a pause.

'You know about Trevor…' There was a pause. 'Of course.' Another pause. 'She's, my sister. We are family.' There was a brief uncomfortable silence then Mary changed the subject to staff rotas.

'I don't like these new rotas… the shifts are too long,' declared Mary.

'Too right,' agreed Daphne. Then the twin interjected.

'You know there's a physical difference between myself and my twin. One of us has green eyes and one of us has blue eyes.' Mary and Daphne glanced at each other in surprise.

'You know what… I never noticed,' said Daphne.

'Yeah, I've got blue eyes and Hyacinth has got green eyes.' Mary and Daphne looked at her eyes and then realised the meaning of what she just said. They had been talking to Deborah, not Hyacinth.

'We thought… you were Hyacinth!' said Mary, feeling totally embarrassed.

'It's ok… a lot of people make the same mistake,' said Deborah.

***

Hyacinth entered the canteen at Talbot's and after buying her coffee she decided, after some hesitation, to join her sister who was sitting alone. She sat down, restrained and civil. There was still tension between the two.

'Hi,' said Hyacinth.

'Hi,' said Deborah.

It was Friday. They both had the weekend off.

'What are you doing over the weekend?' inquired Hyacinth.

'Shopping,' said Deborah.

'Anything exciting?' probed Hyacinth.

Hyacinth had no inkling of what Deborah was going to say next.

'A dress for our engagement party!' declared Deborah.

'You're getting engaged?' Hyacinth paused. She was stunned.

'That's right,' said Deborah coolly. 'Trevor is organising the engagement party.'

Hyacinth sipped her coffee in silence. Her sister's betrayal romance had become a whirlwind romance that would eventually lead the couple straight up the church aisle to exchange wedding vows!

***

The following day at Talbot's supermarket Mary and Daphne were once again joined in the canteen by one of the twins. The twins were deliberately staying apart from one another. Deborah worked as a cashier on the tills, whereas Hyacinth worked in the warehouse.

'Can you pass the sugar Hyacinth,' asked Mary. The latter had deliberately asked this question to confirm the identity of the twin after the previous days' debacle. Mary glanced at Daphne. 'Yesterday we talked to your sister… well, it was very embarrassing because we thought Deborah was you.'

'That happens a lot. 'Hyacinth looked downcast. 'They're getting engaged…'

'They?' inquired Daphne.

'Deborah and my ex-boyfriend. 'Mary and Daphne glanced at each other. 'My sister is a material girl living in a material world. Like Madonna says in the song. She has always been interested in mergers and acquisitions,' declared Deborah cryptically.

Hyacinth.

'How do you mean?' inquired Mary.

'Trevor… my ex. He's a very successful businessman. That's his speciality. Mergers and acquisitions. Trevor's a nice acquisition and their marriage will be a perfect merger. 'Mary and Daphne glanced at each other.

***

It was coming to the close of Talbot's staff meeting. The store manager, Mr Henderson, smiled as he made the following announcement.

'And now some good news. I'm very glad to announce that one of our cashiers Deborah Wendell will be getting engaged. She will be holding an engagement party at Benny's bar on the 24th of August on Portland Pier. Everybody is invited.'

Mary and Daphne, in attendance at this staff meeting, noted that Hyacinth glared at Deborah during this announcement. People dispersed as the meeting ended. Hyacinth approached her sister Deborah.

'Did Trevor ever take you to Ocean Pier? Did he ever say to you let's walk on water?' There was a pause. The two sisters glared at each other, the tension and friction almost unbearable. Deborah remained silent and defiant. Hyacinth continued. 'I thought so because that's what he did with me. 'Hyacinth took her leave, her small frame concealing a simmering rage.

***

Hyacinth was on her break at Talbot's; she was sitting alone in the canteen sipping coffee. Her mind drifted back to the past, when she was at secondary school. She recalled three things. First, during a lesson about the second world war the name of Vyacheslav Molotov captured her attention. Why? A lethal weapon bearing his name was conjured up by Finnish soldiers fighting Soviet tanks. At the time Molotov was the Soviet foreign minister. The weapon called a Molotov cocktail was simple and portable. The weapon consisted of a small bottle containing petrol and a piece of cloth. When lit with a match a ball of flame was created. During her career as an arsonist Hyacinth would deploy this weapon more than once.

The second thing she remembered was a visit to the museum of London. She was mesmerised by newsreel footage of the blitz during the second world war; of a wall of fire encircling St Pauls cathedral. At the museum she also learnt that the V2 rockets that hit London were launched from a forest in Holland. As the rockets ascended, leaving a trail of fire, the surrounding trees were set on fire. The third memory was the day she played truant and was walking down the Woolwich Road. Earlier in the day she had picked up a box of matches from the school playground. She approached a waste bin on the pavement. She stopped and looked inside it. The bin contained an assortment of rubbish including a newspaper. A thought entered her head. She looked around and noticed that there were no other pedestrians on the road, just passing traffic. She pulled out the box of matches and bent over the waste bin, setting the newspaper alight. She then walked away.

She walked to a nearby bus stop and sat down at the bus stop. She watched the small flames coming out of the bin. She was mesmerised. The flames grew larger. Suddenly the fire brigade arrived on the scene. The fireman extinguished the flames in the bin with a water hose. As far as Hyacinth was concerned when he extinguished the flames, he extinguished the fun. It was a moment of self-discovery.

***

One summer, when the twins had turned sixteen, they had an encounter with a fortune teller. A small booth on Ocean pier, larger than a telephone booth, was inhabited by the piers' fortune teller. A woman of advancing years she was a part of the fixtures and fittings of Ocean Pier. Hyacinth and Deborah were strolling along the pier when Deborah grabbed her arm.

'Why don't you get your fortune told?'

'I don't think so,' said Hyacinth defiantly.

'Why not?'

'The fortune teller Agnes. She was born on the 6th of August 1945!' Hyacinth declared, as if this fact ended all debate on the matter.

Deborah looked bemused.

'Why does that matter?' said Deborah.

'Why?' said Hyacinth incredulous. 'The 6th of August 1945 was the day the atom bomb was dropped on Hiroshima! Agnes has got catastrophe hard-wired into her DNA!'

'Go on. What have you got to lose?' persisted Deborah.

Hyacinth sighed and eventually surrendered to her sister's wishes. She pulled away a curtain and saw a small woman sitting on a chair, swathed in scarves. The woman smiled and motioned for Hyacinth to sit down. There was a small table between the chairs.

'What's your name?'

'Hyacinth.'

'An unusual name. A lovely name. Show me your hands, palms upwards. 'She paused, staring at the hands. 'Throughout your life's journey you will be surrounded by light. You have a fierce determination. You will struggle to achieve happiness. Someone close to you will betray you and will hurt you deeply.' She stopped and stared at Hyacinth. 'Some day in the future Ocean pier itself will be destroyed!'

'Well thank you. 'Hyacinth had heard enough, paid the fee and then took her leave. The fortune teller had unnerved her. She re-joined her sister.

'How did it go?' inquired Deborah.

'I told you she foresees catastrophe. The writing is on the wall for Ocean Pier! Let's get out of here!'

***

Watching television at home Hyacinth happened to come across a fascinating programme. Called the one hundred greatest ever gadgets it was presented by a celebrity. The world seemed awash with celebrities. A gadget was defined as a mechanical or electronic device used in everyday life. The gadgets on display were numerous and varied. Some seemed of marginal importance such as the apple peeler. Others seemed much more significant: the kettle, the phone, the computer, the mobile phone, the iPad, the iPhone, the wristwatch, television, the ballpoint pen and the radio. But Hyacinth reflected that on this subject she was ahead of the curve. There was only one winner and she predicted it. An everyday object, often taken for granted, it combined beauty and utility. The lighter, a portable device, generated a small flame. That flame gave Hyacinth an overwhelming feeling of rapture.

***

Hyacinth saw news reports on television about a series of wildfires in Canada caused by lightning. In this country a coffin factory was hit by a bolt of lightning, causing a massive fire. Hyacinth once had a close encounter with lightning when walking through a park. Suddenly a jagged white line hit a tree and severed a branch from the tree, accompanied by a thunderous noise. She was mesmerised by the spectacle afforded by the bolt of lightning and the brief spark of fire it created.

***

Why the pseudonym Dante? Hyacinth had come across the name Dante whilst reading a newspaper article. She was no bookworm and had to google the word. She discovered that the first part of a poem he had written was called Inferno. She immediately associated the word with fire. Hyacinth had a flaw in her make up; she had a moral deficit. She was totally unconcerned by the human consequences of her fires. If somebody had died, she would have dismissed it as collateral damage. But due to sheer luck her fires had caused no deaths.

One day the police would catch up with her. It was only a

matter of time. A part of her due diligence she conducted before a job was first, to do everything to conceal her identity and second to check locations for CCTV. But one day she would make a mistake.

***

Florence expected Hyacinth to be late for her appointment and she was late. She also noted that Hyacinth looked tense. This was no surprise to Florence on account of two facts. First, Hyacinth was a Scorpio (Florence's thinking was heavily influenced by star signs), and second, she knew all about Trevor. Hyacinth lay on the coach, surrounded by images of various tattoos.

'I need you to remove the tattoo of Trevor and the heart,' Hyacinth said sharply.

'Let's have a look,' Florence replied. She studied her upper left arm. 'That's no problem love.'

Florence decided not to engage in frivolous conversation given that the tattoo not only related to a failed romance but also concerned acrimony with Hyacinth's twin sister. Hyacinth remained silent throughout the procedure until the tattoo was removed.

Hyacinth stood up from the coach and looked at Florence intently.

'You know that Trevor kissed me the last time I saw him. That was the kiss of death!' Hyacinth proclaimed dramatically.

***

When Hyacinth first played Deborah at chess, at the tender age of sixteen, she proved victorious. Prior to the game she had done some research and discovered that checkmate could be accomplished in three moves. This involved the queen's pawn, the king's pawn and a diagonal movement by the queen. Deborah was perplexed and astonished by this explosive defeat and thereafter researched various classic chess moves. The twins took the game of chess seriously and Deborah proved a formidable opponent.

Hyacinth kept a chess board and chess pieces in her locker at Talbot's. One lunchtime the twins bumped into each other, whereupon Hyacinth asked her sister if she wanted a game of chess. Deborah accepted. They found a lone table for two in the staff canteen and set out the chess board and chess pieces, whilst sipping their coffees.

As Deborah laid out the chess pieces on the chessboard Hyacinth noticed the lipstick she was wearing.

'I like your lipstick. Purple… it suits you,' said Hyacinth.

'Thanks,' said Deborah.

Both sisters exercised maximum concentration, focusing on the chess board before them. Deborah played aggressively, taking out Hyacinth's knight and bishop early in the game. But Hyacinth recovered. But she despaired when Deborah took her queen. Luckily again Hyacinth mounted a counterattack and took Deborah's queen. In the last act of the game both sisters possessed a castle each and two pawns each.

One of the top classic chess moves was in fact the rook and pawn endgame. Furthermore, Deborah had in fact researched this very chess move and managed to out manoeuvre her twin sister, thereby defeating her.

'Checkmate!' Deborah declared, moving her castle to capture Hyacinth's king.

'Well played,' conceded Hyacinth.

But as far as Hyacinth was concerned this was not the endgame. She had one more move to make, off the chess board.

***

All over the coast of the United Kingdom beautiful, lonely structures jut out into the sea. Piers hoard memories, preserve history and prompt reverie.

For Hyacinth and Deborah, aside from the family memories it evoked, a pier was the dreamy place where romance blossomed. Both Hyacinth and Deborah accepted Trevor's invitation to walk on water on Ocean Pier and then fell under his spell. Hyacinth felt a fierce bitterness when she was told that the engagement party would be held on Portland Pier.

Three days before Deborah's engagement party a fire broke out on Ocean Pier. The fire broke out at night and consumed the entire structure. It created a unique spectacle; orange flames a vivid counterpoint to a dark sky. On that night Hyacinth watched from a safe distance as the fire engulfed the pier. She now realised why she was fascinated by the dripping clock above Benny's bar on the pier. The clock was sending her a message: time was up for Ocean Pier. She was mesmerised by the fire. The scale of the fire thrilled her: flame into being. Ocean Pier was made of wood so was always vulnerable to fire. A huge effort by the Fire Brigade could not save the structure. Fortunately, there were no fatalities.

***

The police investigation into the identity of Dante still did not bear fruit. One witness identified a small woman in the distance. One CCTV image captured a grainy image of a woman. There was no fingerprint or other forensic evidence pointing to a particular individual. When Dante met someone, she always wore a mask. Hyacinth always knew that one day she would be arrested by the police. But for the moment Dante stayed one step ahead of the police.

***

Mary, Daphne and Hyacinth were joined in the staff canteen by Deborah. They had all seen the news reports about Ocean Pier.

'Sorry Deborah… about Ocean Pier,' said Mary sympathetically.

'We're making other arrangements for the engagement party,' she replied quietly. She looked despondent.

'The news report said it was arson,' chipped in Daphne. There was a silence at the table for a couple of minutes.

'It was Dante's inferno!' declared Hyacinth.

Deborah, Mary and Daphne all looked at Hyacinth. She continued.

'It was Dante, that arsonist. I'll bet she burned down the pier. It was Dante's inferno!'

blah ending
longer than it needed to be

The Diary

Adjusting his eyes to the darkness Rob turned on his torch and was jolted by the sight of a room full of mannequins. Lifeless and eerie he was mesmerised by this strange sight. One of the mannequins was dressed up in a purple nightgown. Rob's burglary had taken on an unexpected turn. He had chosen the bungalow hoping it might have hidden treasures. Just released from prison, he had no intention of turning over a new leaf.

He saw a laptop and a diary on a desk. Pointing his torch around the room he could see no other valuables. Unsettled by the eerie atmosphere he decided to cut his losses and made a swift exit with the purloined laptop and diary via the window that afforded his entry.

***

Three months earlier. Daphne and Mary, shop assistants at Talbot's supermarket, were on duty at the self-service tills. In the background, music echoed around the high ceilings of the supermarket. Doing a walkabout was the general manager, Mr Johnson, sharply dressed and erect.

'You've dropped something Mary?'

'Have I?'

'Your smile. Lose that smile and you lose customers!'

'Yes Mr Johnson.'

Daphne and Mary stared at each other. Close friends in their twenties they both enjoyed making wry observations about the people who shopped at Talbot's. That morning, for instance Mary could not help but notice a smart, well-dressed middle-aged man, a shopping basket in his hand, talking to himself. The man noticed Mary staring at him and he approached her.

'I'm an actor. I'm learning my lines!' he said smiling.

'Oh! I see,' said Mary slightly embarrassed.

'Though this be madness yet there is method in it!' He declared in a very actorly way.

'Hamlet!' she declared.

'A scholar and a shop assistant!' he said delighted by her knowledge of the bard. He then took his leave and carried on shopping.

Later, the self-service tills started to become busy. A child was screaming at his mother; he did not like the biscuits she had bought. The mother tried to placate her son; then she became decisive and forceful.

'They'll have to do this week Sam. I'm in a hurry now,' she declared to her son.

At another till the actor who Mary had spoken to earlier was scanning his purchases. He looked at Mary.

'How sharper than a serpent's tooth it is to have a thankless child!' he remarked.

'King Lear!' she retorted.

'Indeed. 'He looked surprised, smiled at Mary and took his leave.

***

Mary and Daphne were working on the self-service tills. Talbot's supermarket was quiet. Daphne showed Mary a text message on her mobile phone. The message was short and brutal. It read: fuck you.

'Who's that from?

'That's from Brian. We've split up.'

'He didn't take it well then.'

'What are you doing after work?'

'I'm going to visit my dad's grave.'

'Want some company?'

'Sure.'

The graveyard covered a large area. Some gravestones were larger and more ornate than others. Daphne pointed in the direction of her dad's gravestone as they approached it. When Daphne and Mary arrived at the gravestone, they were horrified by the sight that confronted them. Somebody had spray painted two words on the gravestone. The words in large white letters were Paedo Scum.

'Oh my God!' exclaimed Daphne.

Mary instinctively held on to Daphne's arm.

'What an awful thing to do. Who could have done it? asked Mary.

'I know who done this. This was no vandal. My dad was no paedophile. This was somebody out for revenge. This was Brian!' she declared decisively.

'What are you going to do?' asked Mary.

'Well first I'm contacting the police. Then I'll ask the man in charge of the cemetery to clean my dad's gravestone,' said Daphne.

Daphne called the police, and they took photographs of the vandalised gravestone. Crucially they found a discarded spray can nearby.

Mary and Daphne were on their break, sipping coffee at Talbots' café a week after the gravestone incident.

'I told you it was Brian who vandalised my dad's gravestone,' declared Daphne.

'That's desecration, you know that, damaging a gravestone,' asserted Mary.

'The police found a spray can nearby and when they checked

the fingerprints on the can they were Brian's. He's been charged with damaging public property. The gravestone has been cleaned,' said Daphne looking relieved.

'What an evil thing to do!' said Mary.

'I've got something for you,' said Daphne.

Daphne removed a small object from her handbag. She gave it to Mary.

'What is it?' inquired Mary.

'A personal alarm. What with this serial rapist on the loose there's no harm in carrying this around with you? So far, he's attacked ten women!' declared Daphne.

'Thanks Daphne. Hopefully I'll never need it.'

***

Mary had been out for a drink with Daphne and her head was swimming with alcohol. On her way home she smiled at the thought that Daphne's last boyfriend was presently a member of the prison population. She got off the bus and noted there was a full moon. She had to walk over the heath in order to get to her flat. The night was quiet. She suddenly sensed there was somebody behind her. She wanted to turn around but was afraid to do so. Then she felt an intense pain on her head. She was seized by powerful hands and pushed into some nearby bushes. Small and plump she was easily overpowered. She had forgotten to put her personal alarm in her handbag. She was at the mercy of a madman. He was wearing a balaclava, a fact that intensified her terror. She waited endlessly for the nightmare to end.

***

Over the weekend Mary did not reply to Daphne's texts. Daphne did not attach any significance to this fact, although Mary always replied to her texts. Then on Sunday evening she received a text from Mary saying that she was in hospital. Alarmed Daphne immediately headed to the hospital. As she approached Mary's bed she saw with horror the gashes on her face. On seeing Daphne Mary burst into tears. Daphne tried to contain herself.

'What happened?'

'I was raped.'

'Oh God!'

'The police are investigating.'

Daphne fell into a silence. She held Mary's hand.

'Did you get a good look at him?

'He was wearing a balaclava. It happened just after I got off the bus.'

'They'll get him Mary.'

***

On release from prison Rob slowly grew accustomed to the wide-open spaces. He regarded the sky as a sublime thing, never to be taken for granted. He admitted that he still got excited when he saw a family packing luggage in their car for a holiday. This meant an empty house. Tall and wiry, he had a slightly crooked face, his jaw tilted to one side. He needed some groceries so went to the supermarket for bread and milk. On entering Talbot's supermarket, he was unaware that his ex-girlfriend Daphne was working there. Daphne presented an unmistakeable Goth presence to the world. She was making her way to the Staff door for her morning break when Rob spotted her. She stopped.

'How are you keeping?' said Rob.

'I'm fine. You're out!'

'Yeah. I got released early for good behaviour.'

'You're going to stay on the right side of the law now!'

'Of course.' He looked distracted. 'Listen, I need to talk to you about something.'

'What?'

'Look I came across something… it doesn't feel right.'

'You know we're over Rob.'

'I know. But I need help with this.'

'I'll meet you at the Coach and Horses later at seven.'

'I know it. Ok.' At that Rob took his leave.

The Coach and Horses was newly refurbished; it had an air of newness, of re-invention. In the background music played, a song by Rick Astley, Never Gonna Give You Up. Rob was sitting at a table drinking a pint of beer. He ordered a drink for her.

'I told you I was never gonna give you up. You gave me up.'

Daphne looked exasperated. He continued. 'Look something happened the other night.'

'Well what is it?'

He looked uncomfortable and glanced around the pub.

'I turned over a house the other night…'

'Jesus Rob!' she said furiously.

'Look the house was full of mannequins!'

'Mannequins?'

'Yes mannequins. There were about ten mannequins in the back room. One of the mannequins was dressed up in a nightie. I sensed something in that house. Something evil. I got out of there double quick.'

'I should report you to the police. 'She paused exasperated.

'I'm going back there this evening, to see who lives there. To observe from the street.'

'What do you want me to do?'

'Come with me. The guy in that house is up to something. And it is a man in that house.'

'Ok. 'She said exasperated, giving in to his request.

***

The street on which the bungalow was located was a quiet suburban street. Rob and Daphne walked up and down the street; they hung around a street corner, trying to look as if they were not watching the bungalow in question. They waited three hours, late afternoon, when a car pulled up outside the bungalow. Rob and Daphne were on other side of the road, some distance from the bungalow. A thick set, well-dressed man in his thirties, got out of the car and entered the bungalow.

'He looks like a professional bloke,' said Rob.

'Well there's your man Rob. He's a professional oddball who likes mannequins. It's not against the law to like mannequins. Anyhow I need to go. I didn't tell you about Mary, did I?'

'What about Mary?'

'She was raped.'

'Oh my God.'

'The police are saying that Mary could be the victim of this serial rapist. So far, he's attacked ten women. All at night in the London area.'

'Did you see the news?'

'No,' said Daphne.

'He's changed his MO as the police say. Yesterday he attacked a girl walking through a park. He was wearing a balaclava!'

'Here's my mobile phone number,' said Daphne, handing him a piece of paper.

She then took her leave.

***

The following morning Rob woke up with a toothache. He rang

the dental clinic, and he was booked in for an emergency appointment. The dental clinic was situated near the soulless council estate where he lived, in a one bed flat. Rob waited for about twenty minutes in the waiting room and then he was called in to the dental room, complete with the large chair underneath sinister dental apparatus and a drill. When he entered the room the dentist had his back to him, as he was studying a computer screen.

'Good morning,' he said breezily.

'Morning,' said Rob.

Rob was keen to get this ordeal over with as quickly as possible so wanted to dispense with the courtesies. However, when the dentist turned around Rob recognised him immediately. He was the man who owned the bungalow. The dentist, a Mr Foster examined his teeth and said that it was a simple matter of a filling that needed to be replaced.

'So first I'll need to give you a small injection to numb your jaw. An important part of my job as a dentist is to relieve the patient of pain.'

Later, Rob would recall these words clearly.

***

Rob rang Daphne on his mobile phone.

Rob: Hi Daphne. It's Rob.

Daphne: Hi Rob.

Rob: I just saw bungalow man.

Daphne: Where?

Rob: I had a toothache. So, I went to the dental clinic near my flat. The dentist who treated me is bungalow man.

Daphne: I wonder what his patients would think if they knew about his mannequins?

***

Henry Foster had agreed to do a bungee jump to raise money for a local hospice. When asked by a journalist for a local newspaper why he was doing it he replied that he wanted to give something back to the community. The bungee jump was to take place from a crane located in south London. The essence of a bungee jump was that a person jumped from a high place, with a body harness strapped to their body, they would descend into the void then when it reached a certain level the descent would abruptly stop, and the person attached to the body harness would be left swinging in the air.

Henry's body harness was checked repeatedly by the safety experts. They eventually gave Henry the thumbs up. Beneath his mild-mannered exterior Henry was fearless. Nothing could harm him. When the moment of truth arrived, Henry propelled himself from the platform at the top of the crane without hesitation. The descent was an enormous shock to his body, as was the sudden stop. At the bottom of the crane, he was released from his safety harness by a team of helpers.

After completing the bungee jump, he was congratulated by the event organisers and was interviewed by the local press. He was feted as a hero.

Henry Foster was a successful, hardworking dentist. Years of study at dental school had paid off and he now earned a good living, his dental work based on fillings and extractions. After setting up his dental practice he decided to give something back to the community and he did some voluntary work for the Samaritans. His colleagues looked up to him with awe.

When asked about his work with the Samaritans he said, 'I listen to troubled souls crying out for help.'

He lived alone, out on the edge of London, in a small bungalow. He was once engaged to be married, but the relationship collapsed. Truth be told, his colleagues in the dental practice knew little of the man Henry Foster.

At home in his bungalow his wardrobe in his bedroom was neatly arranged: shirts and trousers hanging in separate spaces of his wardrobe and socks, underwear and pullovers in separate compartments of his wardrobe. His wardrobe mirrored his brain: ordered and methodical.

Henry was a man attached to his routines so when his car malfunctioned, and he had to take the train to work he was annoyed. He had some administrative work to do so he had to work late. Arriving, at his local train station he ascended the stairs for the exit. The stairway was empty except for a young woman. As he ascended the stairs, he accidentally brushed against the young woman walking up the stairs at the same time. She uttered the words,' Excuse me,' clearly angered by the incident. Henry felt a sudden surge of rage, turned around and kicked the woman in the chest, propelling her down the stairs.

He then carried on walking, unperturbed and composed. He did not turn around to see if the woman was ok. Out of his sight the woman picked herself up from the bottom of the stairs, bruised and dazed. A subsequent police investigation could not identify the attacker and came to nothing. This was another random act of violence by a faceless lunatic in anonymous London. Scratch the surface of the civilised urban man and sometimes there was a naked brute underneath.

***

At the dental clinic where Henry worked, an administrative mistake caused confusion in patient bookings. Normally Henry would shrug this off but, on this day, Henry spoke sharply to the clerical staff and at one point shouted aggressively at staff. This was out of character and noted by his staff. But the real reason for his agitation had nothing to do with the dental clinic. The real reason was the discovery that there was a break-in at his bungalow and during this break-in two of his personal items were stolen. He had no idea who had stolen them or where they were.

***

It was Daphne's day off so she decided to take her early morning jog. She did her running in some nearby ancient woodlands. She liked the stillness and quiet of the woodlands. She followed a twisting path, that in places was flanked by huge oak trees. The huge oak trees were the silent guardians of the woodlands.

While running she thought about her friend Mary. The previous night she tried to ring her, but Mary did not answer her phone. She knew that Mary was in a deep depression. Suddenly some bushes moved, and a brown four-legged creature ran out on to the path. She initially thought it was a fox, but it was in fact a small deer. Then a small head popped up from some bushes and stared, with its huge eyes, at Daphne. This was another small deer and seconds later it too had disappeared.

She continued her run but started to feel uneasy. She thought she was alone in the woods, but she sensed that somebody was watching her. She looked around, stopping in order to do so. She saw no one. She started to run again, but this time she distinctly heard the rustle of bushes behind her. She stopped and swivelled around. She tightened the grip on her personal alarm. Again, she saw no one. She was sweating profusely. She was now seized with fear. She turned around and ran as fast as she could until she reached the boundary of the woodlands and the path that led to the main road.

***

Debbie, the receptionist at Henry Fosters dental clinic, was tidying up the reception area before departing for home. Henry came into the reception area to ask her if she could alter her rota slightly. She agreed. She put her coat on and checked her pockets. She fished out a personal alarm.

'Is that a personal alarm?' inquired Henry.

'Yes. What with this rapist out there I feel better with this. He's attacked ten women you know.'

'Oh those women were just roadkill!' Henry said laughing.

Debbie stopped and stared at Henry. She had heard him

correctly. He described rape victims as roadkill. She was appalled but at the same time she was aware that Henry was her boss. So, she said nothing, but it confirmed her view that her boss was a very strange man indeed.

'I'm just kidding Debbie. Sorry I am insensitive sometimes.'

'Goodnight, Henry.'

'Goodnight, Debbie.'

Debbie then took her leave.

***

Daphne was working on the self-service tills at Talbot's. Mary was on sick leave. The self-service tills were busy. A thick set, middle-aged man required some help on the self-service till. Daphne approached to help; when he turned around, she recognised him immediately. It was the man who she and Rob observed enter the bungalow, the other evening. He was polite and smiled at her flirtatiously. Indeed, there was something distinctly creepy about the man. He had no idea that she was a party to his secret yearning for mannequins. Daphne now felt like a detective, a keeper of secrets.

***

A famous philosopher once said that the night sky is one of the noblest spectacles to the human senses. But Henry Foster used the night sky as a starry canvas under which he stalked and attacked innocent women. After these malevolent night-time excursions, he returned to his house and then caressed lovingly his mannequins.

Creepy bastard.

***

Rob rang Daphne and asked her if she wanted to go to the funfair on the heath. She agreed although she was intent on keeping things between her and Rob at the level of friendship. She told him that there was an invisible line between the two of them and that he was not to cross that line. She told him that she saw the man who entered the bungalow at Talbot's supermarket. She added that he gave her the creeps.

The funfair was a swirl of noise and colour. The funfair attracted a crowd of people, mainly young, craving excitement and diversion. Food stands emitted the smell of fried food. Carousals, dodgems, the Ferris wheel, the tunnel of love and the hall of mirrors were available to everybody. Daphne bought a burger in a bun for both herself and Rob.

They saw a coconut shy stall. The object of the exercise was to throw a ball at a coconut positioned on the top of a pole. There was a total of three coconuts. Rob and Daphne looked at each other and Rob said he would have a go. He smiled at Daphne, and she was taken aback by his confidence. He threw the first ball and hit the coconut; he threw the second coconut and hit the coconut; and the process was repeated with the last coconut. The stall holder gave him the three coconuts in a bag. Then he revealed a pertinent fact about his skill at throwing objects.

'You know that I once worked in a circus,' said Rob.

'No, I didn't know that,' she replied.

'I helped at first setting up the tent, manual work then I did some training knife throwing.'

'You're kidding!'

'Absolutely true. I never had a knife throwing act, but the circus knife thrower said I was a natural. But I never had the nerve to do a knife throwing act with a real person, I was afraid I might kill somebody. Then when the circus moved on, I drifted into a life of crime. 'He paused. 'How's Mary?'

'Not great. She's depressed. Let's go into the hall of mirrors!'

Rob and Daphne walked along a corridor of mirrors, unable to avoid their reflections. At the end of the corridor, they came to a circular open area, dominated by mirrors. The whole experience was unnerving and disorientating. Other people milled around, staring into the mirrors, mesmerised. Daphne stared into the mirror, and behind her saw the man from the bungalow, standing still, watching her. She looked at the man, in the mirror, for a good fifty to sixty seconds. When she turned around, he was gone like a phantom.

'Did you see him?' she asked Rob.

'See who?' he said looking confused.

'The man from the bungalow. He was here, staring at me!'

'Well he's not here now.'

They left the hall of mirrors. Daphne was anxious and unnerved.

'You know I do my running in the woodland near my flat. Well yesterday morning I thought there was someone in the woods watching me. I know a man was there watching me.'

'Are you sure?'

'I'm sure. I'm not being paranoid. 'She paused. 'Well, I'm not going to be scared off by this rapist. Tomorrow I'm doing my run as usual.'

'Look. Before you go, I've a favour to ask. I want to show you something.'

'What?'

'A diary. You know with my dyslexia I have a problem reading.'

'A diary? What's so special about that?'

'Well I took it from the bungalow.'

'What! You mean you want me to look at some stolen property?'

'Yeah. Look there's something odd about the diary. It's in my flat. It won't take long to have a look at it.'

Daphne sighed but agreed to look at the diary. When they arrived at Rob's flat it was in an extreme state of disorder. The settee and armchair were old and torn; the walls needed re-painting;

clothes were strewn over chairs; the carpet was discoloured; newspapers and cans of beer were discarded on the floor and the rubbish bin in the kitchen was overflowing and needed emptying.

'Sorry about the state of the flat,' Rob said sheepishly. 'Sit down, I'll get the diary. 'He fetched the diary from a small brown wooden cabinet and gave it to Daphne.

She opened the diary and noted that there were a series of dates and next to the dates we entries. The handwriting was clear and easy to read. One entry read as follows. Daphne read out the entry to Rob.

10 May. Followed the subject down the high street. She did not realise I was following her. Small and thin; in her twenties. At one point she got something out of her handbag and inserted it in her mouth. I think it was an inhaler. She turned down an alleyway adjacent to the railway line. She was all alone, and the alleyway was poorly lit. Perfect. I rushed her and hit her over the head. Still conscious she pleaded,' Don't hurt me. I did what I had to do and then made off.'

Daphne stopped reading and looked at Rob.

'My God. He's a rapist,' declared Rob.

'There's more dates here. Listen 6th June. Followed girl out of railway station. But I made a mistake. She realised that I was following her and ran off. Luckily, I don't think she made a report to police. Also, the lighting was poor so she didn't get a good look at me.' Daphne paused. 'Let me check these dates against the dates when the serial rapist struck.'

Daphne produced her smartphone and began to search for information and dates about the serial rapist. She checked the dates in the diary and the dates on her smartphone about the list of rapes.

'Well?' inquired Rob eagerly.

'Rob. The dates they match. 3rd January 26th January 10 February 23rd February 10th May 23 May 23rd June 11th April 7th January 26th January. 'She looked up at Rob. 'He's a monster. He's the serial rapist!’ Her eyes continued to scan the diary. Tears welled up in her eyes. ‘Oh my God. Listen to this entry dated June 11th. Followed small plump girl off the bus. ‘She stopped reading the diary entry.

‘What’s the matter?’

‘June 11th. The girl he followed off the bus. That was Mary!’

Stunned into silence there was a long pause. Then Daphne made a declaration.

‘You must take this to the police. He is the serial rapist! And he raped Mary.’

‘If I take that diary to the police I’ll be charged with burglary.’

Daphne stood up and glared at Rob.

‘If you don’t take that diary to the police I will!’

She then took her leave. author likes this phrase

***

The woods were normally quiet but this morning the eerie growl of a deer permeated the area. Daphne followed her normal running route; the growl of the deer was somewhere in the distance. Everything was still. But she still could not shake off the feeling she was being watched. She reached a curve in the path that was flanked by huge oak trees and high bushes. Suddenly she heard the noise of a twig being broken. Then she sensed something moving toward her from behind. She felt an intense pain on her head and then she was grabbed by a powerful pair of hands.

A stocky man, average height, wearing a balaclava, had jumped out from behind bushes and hit her on the head with a piece of wood. He then began to pull her in the bushes.

Out of nowhere a man shouted,’ Stop!’ A couple of yards away stood Rob. He pulled a knife from his pocket and threw it at the attacker. His aim was sure and true. Rob had deliberately targeted his leg. The knife embedded itself on the thigh of his right leg.

The attacker screamed in pain. He managed to hobble, moving away as fast as he could. Rob went to aid Daphne. She was stunned and barely conscious. Rob held her in his arms.

'I told you I was good at knife throwing! he declared. 'When you told me the other day you were going jogging in these woods, I had a sixth sense you might be in danger, so I decided to follow you. 'He paused. 'I'm giving the diary to the police.'

He produced a mobile phone from his pocket and called for the police and an ambulance. Whilst an ambulance took Daphne to hospital, accompanied by Rob, the police searched the woods, and arrested her attacker. It was indeed Henry Foster.

Great - loved it to be longer.

The Architect

'I'm eighteen you know… but I'm never going to make it to nineteen!'

Mary, the shop assistant at Talbot's supermarket, stared at the young woman when she made this extraordinary statement. 'The young woman had an angelic appearance, like a face in a classic painting. She had a faraway look in her eyes.' She continued:

'There's something coming toward me.' Then the young woman took off with the vegan dish she had collected from the shelves. Mary felt like a priest who had just heard a confession; only that this confession was heard in the middle of a supermarket.

A few minutes earlier the young woman had asked Mary where the vegan dishes were located, and Mary had shown her. Talbot's was a large supermarket, Mary a young member of staff in her early twenties. The words of the young woman reverberated in her head,' I'll never make nineteen… there's something coming toward me.'

Mary walked back to the self-service section where she normally worked. Her friend Daphne was working there. Daphne, splendid in her Goth make-up and her black boots; Mary small and plump, a ball of energy. Their imaginations filled with science fiction and supernatural stories; they were always on the lookout for strange occurrences. They were two innocents parachuted into a malign world.

'Something weird just happened. 'Daphne's eyes lit up. 'That girl I just helped… she told me she was eighteen, and then she said she'd never make nineteen!'

'Wow.' Daphne paused to think. 'She might have had a premonition… that something terrible was going to happen.'

'Daphne I've got a feeling we've not heard the last of that girl.'

'The deadwood stage is rolling on over the plains,' said Daphne a reference to the famous Doris Day song. They were now on a mission to inquire, probe, investigate. Mary and Daphne's curiosity would take them to the ends of the earth.

***

Mary and Daphne were sipping coffee in Talbot's staff canteen.

'Have you seen the new member of staff,' Daphne inquired.

'No,' said Mary.

'There she is over there,' she said looking at the farthest end of the room.

The new member of staff was young and had a face that did not look quite natural; her cheeks were smooth and plumped up as if she had a facelift.

Mary studied her face and felt sure she had seen her face before. There was something that jarred.

'I've seen her somewhere before,' Mary said, a perplexed tone to her voice. She continued,' Why would a young woman like that get a facelift?'

'You reckon that she's had a facelift?'

'Definitely,' declared Mary.

'Mind you Kim Kardashians' had a facelift and she's young and beautiful.'

Mary continued to study the newcomer's face.

'Good God I know who she is. Remember that abduction and murder of two girls a couple of years ago by a lorry driver?'

'Yeah, I remember that,' said Daphne.

'Remember the girlfriend was arrested. The police suspected her involvement in the crime but could not prove it, although she got done for perverting the course of justice. Well, she's the girlfriend. And she's had a facelift to disguise her identity.'

'Wow, I think your right!' exclaimed Daphne.

Afterward Mary approached the manager of Talbot's David Henderson. Brisk and business-like Mr Henderson did not waste time with small talk.

'See that new member of staff Doreen Hazell… well she's not who she says she is!'

'What do you mean?' he fired back brusquely.

'That's a fictitious name, not her real name,' Mary declared.

'Oh really… and how do you know that?'

'Because I watch the news,' she replied confidently.

'And who is she really?' he said with a mixture of scepticism and sarcasm.

'Her name is Tina Martin. She and her boyfriend were arrested by the police regarding the abduction and murder of two girls…'

'You can't be serious?'

'Although she wasn't charged with those crimes she got done for perverting the course of justice. She's been given a new identity by the police and she's had facial surgery to disguise her identity.'

David Henderson looked stunned.

'I'll investigate it.'

Then Mary left his office.

***

The following day at Talbot's supermarket it was evident that the new member of staff Doreen Hazell had not turned up for work. The manager Mr Henderson reported to staff that she would not be returning to work and would not elaborate as to why. Mary and Daphne's suspicions were confirmed.

Meanwhile Daphne had read a disturbing report in the newspaper; that a young woman had gone missing. Daphne produced a copy of the newspaper in the staff canteen and showed Mary a photo image of the woman.

'My God it's her… the young woman who spoke to me the other day!'

'Spooky,' said Daphne.

'Something terrible has happened to that woman!' declared Mary.

***

Later that day, whilst working on the self-service till Mary and Daphne noticed Rasputin enter the supermarket. Daphne once saw a film about Rasputin and felt that this customer was a dead ringer. He was tall, had long dark hair flowing to his shoulders and had an intimidating presence. But the physical characteristic that dwarfed all others were his eyes. Blazing, penetrating, staring, mad, no adjective quite captured their unique intensity. Mary had once assisted him locate a product and had never forgotten those other worldly eyes.

Another regular Talbot's customer, a police officer, entered the store and stopped to help an old lady who had dropped her shopping bag, causing her groceries to scatter all over the floor. The old lady thanked him. The police officer was always smiling and personable. Walking past the self-service tills he greeted Mary.

'All quiet… No trouble?'

'Everything's fine,' she responded.

'Just to give you a head up there's been a spike in burglaries in the local area so you might want to check out all the locks on your windows and doors. We've got a special unit working on burglaries.'

'Oh thanks for the advice.'

He then moved off and to Mary and Daphne's surprise he began to strike up a conversation with Rasputin.

'So Rasputin has got a friend.'

'And he's a police officer!'

'Those eyes of his sent chills down my spine,' declared Mary.

'You do know that Rasputin had superhuman strength. They had a hell of a job killing him…'

'Who's they?' inquired Mary.

'Well, he became very close with the wife of the tsar of Russia during the nineteenth century… he had this hold over her… so, the people around the tsar decided to bump him off. They stabbed him, shot him… but he took ages to die. So, if he kicks off Charlie at security will need back up,' asserted Daphne.

Suddenly Mary and Daphne noticed Rasputin fall to the floor. The police officer, standing next to him, stepped back and then walked off rapidly. Indeed, you could say he fled the scene. Mary and Daphne were at Rasputin's side in seconds. Mary checked his breathing and pulse whilst Daphne pulled out her phone to summon an ambulance.

When the ambulance arrived the paramedics, with some difficulty, put him on a stretcher and took him away to hospital. It appeared he suffered a seizure. Whilst the paramedics were putting Rasputin on the stretcher Mary noticed a letter, under a shelf on the floor, adjacent to where Rasputin had fallen. She picked it up and put it in her pocket knowing that it almost certainly belonged to Rasputin.

In the staff canteen Mary opened the letter.

'I found this letter near Rasputin,' Mary whispered, looking around nervously. 'It's a gas bill. Rasputin's' name is Andrew Roberts. And we have his address.'

'What should we do?'

'He's up to something wicked, I just know it. I say we check out the house.'

'Yeah. The deadwood stage is rolling on over the plains.'

***

Mardell Pharmacy served the local community for decades. Pamela, a young pharmacy assistant, had worked their twelve months. She was happy in her job and the manager had come to depend on her hard work and reliabilty. But there was one issue that upset her and she had decided to broach the subject with her boss.

The issue was one of the customers, Andrew Roberts. Pamela was terrified of him. Once she was in the pharmacy, checking the stock behind the counter, with her back to the shop when the front door to the pharmacy opened. Pamela knew instantly that Andrew Roberts had entered the pharmacy. The impact of his physical presence was immediately felt by Pamela.

Mr. Roberts attended the pharmacy every month to pick up his medicines. Pamela noted that one of his medicines was an anti-depressant. When she served him at the counter she did everything she could to avoid his eyes. Her boss, Mr. Parry listened sympathetically to her concern. He had some good news, however. From next month, Mr Roberts' medicines would be delivered to his house. Pamela breathed a sigh of relief.

The next day Pamela made her way to the pharmacy as usual. Her route took her past Mr Roberts' large Gothic house. As she walked past the house a shiver went down her spine.

***

Andrew Roberts, an ambitious architect, always revered John Tresham's architectural masterpiece The Triangular Lodge. Built in the sixteenth century in Northamptonshire this unique building was a symbolic expression of his Catholic faith. This was a time when it was illegal to practice Catholicism in Protestant England. Tresham was imprisoned for his Catholic faith. The building contained secret messages in line with his Catholic faith. Tresham focused on the number three; this represented the Holy Trinity, God, Christ and the Holy Spirit. The Triangular Lodge was a three-sided building, consisting of three windows on each side of each wall. Each window was capped by a gable. The building had three floors.

When Andrew Roberts first saw The Triangular Lodge, he was mesmerised by its symmetrical beauty. He determined to emulate Tresham and design a similar building of his own. He received a commission from the local authority to design an architectural landmark for the local park. He gladly accepted and called it The Eternal Triangle.

Whilst his professional life was flourishing his personal life disintegrated. He discovered that his wife was having an affair, and this led eventually to the collapse of his marriage. Whilst he was designing the Eternal Triangle, he was the victim of another type of triangle, a romantic triangle, that dripped with deception and betrayal. He often thought of the perverse symmetry of the situation.

As a young man Andrew Roberts' formidable intellect intimidated not only his peers but also his mother and father. He also harboured a chilling secret: he took a perverse pleasure in torturing animals.

Andrew Roberts always caused a sense of unease amongst his colleagues. Many of his colleagues found his peculiar and unique presence sinister. He had deep-set eyes. He seldom smiled. His face appeared devoid of humanity and humour. One of his secretaries resigned because she feared him.

***

Michelle Young, an experienced psychiatrist of ten years standing, was struggling to read her notes about the patient sitting in front of her. She was sitting in an armchair opposite her patient, who was sitting in a similar armchair. He sat there impassively, like a huge eagle. The stark truth was that he unnerved her, hence her problem concentrating. She read that he was diagnosed with clinical depression.

'Andrew, you're an architect. I see you designed The Eternal Triangle… that's in a park nearby isn't it?'

'Yes.'

'So, how are you feeling? I see you were admitted to hospital recently after a seizure.'

'I'm fine.'

'Any problems sleeping?'

'Yes. Thoughts in my head tend to race.'

'I can prescribe some sleeping tablets. Have you had any suicidal thoughts lately?'

'Sometimes.'

'Have the suicidal thoughts increased or decreased?'

'Decreased. When I have a suicidal thought I sometimes go out for a walk.'

'Walking helps?'

'Yes.'

'And the anti-depressant tablet, any side-effects?'

'No. Each day I wake up, look out the window and study the architecture of the clouds in the sky.' He paused, then said impatiently. 'Listen… I need to go. Can you write out my prescription?'

'Certainly.'

She wrote out his prescription and handed it to him. She momentarily caught his eye and took in an intake of breath. She watched him leave with a sigh of relief. She reflected: he was an iceberg. She had no idea what was going on below the water line.

When asked about his suicidal thoughts Andrew Roberts failed to mention the macabre apparatus in his upstairs spare room.

***

Mary reported to the police that she had encountered the missing young woman in Talbot's supermarket just before she disappeared.

She read in the newspapers that she was the second young woman to go missing in the last year.

Daphne had googled the name Andrew Roberts and discovered that there was an architect of the same name. Mary and Daphne were in the canteen at Talbots supermarket.

'So Andrew Roberts could be an architect,' opined Mary.

'Yeah, and I found out something else. There's a small building in a nearby local park called the Eternal Triangle that was designed by Andrew Roberts. It's open to public viewing!'

'Let's go and see it!'

A couple of days later they decided to view the Eternal Triangle. They had to arrange the viewing with the council. The Eternal Triangle had smaller dimensions than the building that inspired it, namely The Triangular Lodge. It had three sides, each wall containing a triangular window. Each wall was capped by a gable. The building had one floor. The council official, a small man continually wiping his nose with a tissue, opened the door with a key. Mary and Daphne walked into a room made from stone. The floor consisted of stone slabs. A wooden table and two wooden chairs occupied the central space. The room was well lit, light pouring in from the three triangular windows. Above each window was a gargoyle, their faces contorted into a horrible shape.

'Spooky!' exclaimed Daphne.

'Very spooky!' Agreed Mary. Both Mary and Daphne walked around the room and stared at the gargoyles. They then took their leave.

***

Mary and Daphne located Rasputin's house later that evening. A large, detached house, it looked like it had a basement. Flanking the front door were two small statues of lions. The door knocker was a snake's head. The front garden was slightly overgrown with grass. The house was creepy.

'What do we do now?' asked Daphne.

'Well I say we break in!'

'That's' illegal!'

'We've got to!' declared Mary.

***

Mary and Daphne were standing on a street corner, across the road from Rasputin's' house. Mary noticed a taxi pull up outside Rasputin's house. Daphne turned to look at the taxi and then she looked at Mary.

'Talk of the devil…' exclaimed Daphne.

The unmistakeable figure of Rasputin exited the taxi, closely followed by a young woman. They both entered the house.

'Wait a minute… that woman he's with. She looks familiar.' Mary paused, thinking. 'That's Doreen Hazell… the new member of staff at Talbots!'

'You're right,' said Daphne, staring at Mary in astonishment. 'Do you understand that?'

'No, I don't. We'll come back later… to find out what's going on in that house.'

***

A day later Mary and Daphne both had a day off and decided that they would keep an eye on Rasputin's house. In effect they were a two-person surveillance unit. Standing on the other side of the road at a discreet distance they noticed the front door open and Rasputin and another man, well-built and stocky, leave the house together. Mary and Daphne both recognised the other man; it was the policeman who came into Talbot's, out of uniform. They both walked off together up the street.

Mary and Daphne looked at each other; they had to seize the moment.

'This is madness!' exclaimed Daphne.

'This is madness! So let's do it!'

They approached the house and moved to the side-gate that was open. This gave access to the rear garden. The garden was in a state of some disorder; overgrown grass was littered with tyres and old pieces of furniture. There was a general air of decay, a dead cat lay on the grass. At the lowest level of the house there was a small window that was boarded up with a piece of wood. There was another window adjacent to the garden that led to the kitchen. It was not locked. Mary opened the window and lifted herself up into the open space then edged herself into the kitchen; Daphne followed suit.

The kitchen smelt stale, dirty dishes in the sink. They entered the hallway; the décor was drab and dull. There was a dining room with a table and chairs; there were no ornaments or family photographs. In the front room both Mary and Daphne's eyes focused on the antique weaponry on the walls, a pistol, a shotgun and a crossbow.

In the hallway there was two sets of stairways: one going to the upper level and one set of stairs going to the basement. They decided to go upstairs. There were three doors. One door led to a bathroom, one to a bedroom but the third door was like a portal to another world. When Mary opened the door, they were confronted by the sight of a large rope, attached to a horizontal beam across the ceiling, arranged in a hangman's noose. The room was bare of furniture except for a single wooden chair. Mary and Daphne looked at one another.

'Let's get out of here!' exclaimed Daphne.

They rushed down the stairs. Mary looked down the second set of stairs, that led to the basement. At the bottom of the stairs, she saw a door that appeared to be made from metal.

'I'm getting out. He might come back,' exclaimed Daphne again, desperate to get out of the house.

'Ok,' said Mary in a hesitating manner. They rushed to the

kitchen and as they wedged themselves through the window, they heard footsteps at the front door. Mary scrambled to get out of the window and closed it behind her as somebody entered the front door. Unseen they both moved away from the house.

***

The plan was simple. Peter had selected the location carefully, woods near the town centre. It was secluded and unpeopled. Andrew would lay prostrate on the ground, under the pretence that he had suddenly became ill and collapsed. Peter would kneel over him applying first aid. Then Peter, a police officer, would summon help from the passing young woman. When the passing young woman knelt to help, Andrew suddenly sprang into life and he and Peter, knocked her unconscious and bundled the young woman into the nearby car. They then took her to a nearby house, the abduction complete.

Nearly everybody trusted a policeman. The only thing was that Peter was not a policeman. The whole thing was a brilliant and daring deception. Ten years before Peter had obtained a police uniform from somebody renowned for illegal transactions. He began to wear the uniform, a good distance from where he lived, so that nobody recognised him. People smiled at him, said hello and asked him for directions. It conferred an authority on him. Peter was unemployed, living on social security payments. He had a criminal conviction for fraud. Peter used the police uniform to fulfil his sick fantasies.

He had met Andrew by chance whilst waiting to see a doctor in hospital. They fell into conversation, and it was soon apparent that they shared the same sick fantasies.

Andrew had met a woman, Tina Roberts, who was involved in covering up the murders of two girls. Tina lived next to Andrew, and they were both attracted to one another. But then Tina's real identity was rumbled, at Talbot's supermarket where she worked, and she had to move to another address.

Andrew was furious with Peter after falling ill in Talbot's

supermarket. Peter explained that he had no choice but to make a quick exit otherwise his deception as a fake policeman may be uncovered.

***

Mary and Daphne were still shaken at what they saw in Rasputin's' house. They were both on duty at the self-service section.

'We've got to go back to the house and check the basement. There's something very wrong in that house. There's something or someone in that basement,' declared Mary.

'I've got a day off tomorrow,' said Daphne.

Suddenly there was a commotion near the supermarket entrance. Three police officers had surrounded a man and were putting him in handcuffs. Charlie, the security guard, was standing next to the police officers. The man being handcuffed was offering no resistance. He was led away to a police car by the police.

During their break Mary and Daphne approached Charlie (nicknamed pitbull because of his physical appearance) and asked him about the incident.

'You know that policeman that comes in here... stocky, friendly?'

'Yeah,' said Mary. Daphne nodded.

'Well it turns out he's not a policeman at all. They arrested him for impersonating a police officer.'

Mary and Daphne turned and looked at each other in astonishment.

***

Mary and Daphne watched Rasputin's' house from the other side of the road. They had to make sure that he was not in the house before they attempted to access the house. They had been there about an hour when the front door of the house opened and the immense figure of Rasputin loomed, a man who could strike fear in the sternest of hearts. Mary and Daphne stepped back, retreating into a nearby bus stop so that they would not be seen. The sun in the sky retreated behind a cloud. They watched him walk down the street; then they walked across the road and approached the house.

They went through the side-gate, walked through the rear garden until they came to the kitchen window. A black cat on the grass near the house watched them and then scurried off. Hearts racing, they both began to perspire. They were pushing their own bravery to its absolute limit. Once they entered the house any scenario was possible. The kitchen window was open; they both lifted themselves up and wedged themselves into the kitchen.

They walked into the hallway and saw the stairway down to the basement. They walked down the stairs until they came to the large door. To the side of the door was a key attached to a piece of string hanging on a nail. Mary knocked on the door.

'Hello. Is there anybody there?'

'Help me. I've been kidnapped!'

'I'm just opening the door.' Mary unlocked the door with the key. She was confronted by a young girl, drawn, pale and unkempt. She recognised the girl immediately as the same girl who spoke to her in the supermarket, and she matched the photo of the girl who went missing. She rushed to Mary and grabbed her desperately.

'I'm Sandra Dee. The big man and the policeman kidnapped me. I've been drugged… a woman comes and gives me a drug that makes me sleepy…' Daphne interjected.

'A woman! Doreen Hazell,' Daphne glanced at Mary.

'I've been attacked. You must call the police.' The look of terror in her eyes were unforgettable.

Daphne pulled out her mobile phone. Daphne phoned the police, said that they had found the missing girl and that she had been kidnapped by Andrew Roberts and that they were presently in the basement of his house in Sun Road. At that moment they heard the front door open; there was a pause. The three women fell silent; the police officer on the phone said that they were on their way.

'Lock the door!' the woman screamed.

Mary rushed to the door and locked the door from the inside with the key. All three-woman stood still and looked at each other, the atmosphere toxic with fear. Suddenly footsteps rushed down the stairs. Somebody on the other side of the door grabbed the door handle.

'Open the door or I'll kill you!' a male voice screamed from the other side of the door. This was Rasputin.

The captive woman grabbed Daphne. Suddenly Rasputin began to hurl his body against the door; the massive thudding sound sent chills down the spines of the three women. Minutes passed that felt like an eternity. Then the police officer on the phone told Daphne that the police car had just arrived at the house.

The three women heard the front door being smashed in by the police. They heard the police screaming,' Armed police… Andrew Roberts surrender yourself!'

Rasputin (real name Andrew Roberts) knew that one day the police would catch up with his crimes. But he had determined that he would never go to prison. He had devised a simple plan to avoid prison. The plan required the ability to endure pain and the ability to confront the ultimate fear. Now was the moment to implement that plan.

The police had nearly broken down the front door. He ran upstairs and opened the door to the spare room. He positioned the wooden chair under the hangman's noose, stood on the chair and arranged the noose around his neck. He then jumped off the chair. Sixty seconds later the police broke down the front door, a group of police officers rushing up the stairs. When the police entered the spare room, they saw Andrew Roberts' limb body swinging backwards and forwards on the end of a rope.

Mary decided to unlock the door and was met by several police officers. Sandra Dee, weeping, was escorted by police out of the building into a waiting car. Before she did so she smiled at Mary and Daphne. Mary and Daphne smiled at each other and held each other's hand. Mary asked one of the police officers what happened to Andrew Roberts?

'When we broke down the front door he rushed upstairs and hanged himself. He had a hangman's noose in the spare room all ready and waiting for himself.'

***

The following day Mary and Daphne were sipping coffee in Talbot's canteen. News reports about Andrew Roberts revealed some horrific revelations.

'So Rasputin wrote a last testament. He'd already abducted and murdered two women before he abducted Sandra Dee… and he was going to make her victim number three,' exclaimed Daphne.

'Apparently, his wife left him for another man years ago. But we were right about the Eternal Triangle. A very spooky place. As the architect he had his own key to the building. What nobody realised when they visited the Eternal Triangle was that two women were buried under the stone slabs. Everybody thought it was just a beautiful piece of architecture… when it was also a mausoleum.'

Really good enjoyed.

The Train Driver

Elvis Presley was everywhere. Or rather Elvis Presley lookalikes were everywhere. Aisle nine, aisle twenty, aisle thirteen, aisle eleven Elvis filled the aisles at Talbot's supermarket. Mary and Daphne, two twenty-something store assistants, watched in wonder at this visual feast. The white suit, the high collar, the dark coiffed hair they all had the same look. Some looked more like Elvis than others.

Mary and Daphne were working at their usual spot, at the self-service tills. After finishing his transaction on the till, one Elvis lookalike turned to Mary and Daphne and delivered the immortal words in an American accent:

'Thank you very much.'

Another Elvis lookalike entered the self-service area. At that moment, the store security guard Terry walked past the self-service area. The ex-wrestler said hello to Mary and Daphne. Then he spotted the Elvis lookalike and stopped in his tracks.

'Peter?' The Elvis lookalike stopped and looked up from the till.

'Terry!' They greeted each other warmly. Terry entered the self-service area smiling broadly.

'Wow. You look… just like Elvis!' exclaimed Terry.

'Just a hobby of mine. There's an Elvis Presley convention. As you can see there's loads of us,' he stated and laughed. 'And I got married a month ago.'

'Congratulations!' Terry exclaimed. He turned to Mary and Daphne. 'This is Peter, a train driver!'

All four laughed, Mary and Daphne greeting him warmly. Peter picked up his shopping.

'Anyhow, I've got to re-join the convention. Good luck,' said Peter.

'Good luck,' said Terry and Peter took his leave. Terry turned to Mary and Daphne. 'Elvis has left the building!' Mary and Daphne both laughed.

***

Peter loved his wife, loved Elvis Presley and was totally committed to his job as a train driver. He possessed a tall bulky frame and had a striking resemblance to his legendary hero. A half glass full type of guy he loved a good joke and was never morose. He and Tina his wife were two peas in a pod. Their relationship was uncomplicated. They held hands in public and left I love you notes to each other on the table nearly every day. They had been married a year now and their love for each other had not diminished.

Peter was one of an army of silent train drivers that drove trains up and down the rail network. Shadowy figures you occasionally caught a fleeting glimpse of their face as a train slowed down on entering a station.

On that fateful Monday he had left Tina a I love You note with a comic flourish: Elvis has left the building. Train drivers have two fears: first making a mistake that leads to a train crash. The second fear was realised on that Monday. He was driving his train; he had just pulled out of a station. For a couple of seconds, he thought he was trapped in a dream or rather a nightmare. From the left, standing near the railway line, he saw a young man. Suddenly he jumped in front of the train. Horror stricken Peter applied the brakes. The young man was killed instantly. At speed it takes a train a mile to stop when the brakes are applied. When the train came to a stop, he alerted the railway network of the incident then jumped out of the cabin and ran back to the location where the young man jumped. The spectacle that greeted him was so gruesome that he vomited at the side of the railway line.

***

Peter's manager ordered him a taxi home. The man who left the house that afternoon for work was a different man to the man returning to the house now. He opened the front door and walked into the kitchen. His wife was at the kitchen table drinking a cup of coffee. As soon as she saw her husband, his face had a deathly pallor, she knew there was something wrong. They stared at each other momentarily.

'I killed a human being today,' he said matter of factly.

'Oh my God!' she replied.

'He jumped in front of the train!' he continued. Tina stood up and embraced her stricken husband.

***

Mary and Daphne were in the staff canteen, enjoying their break from the busy shopfloor at Talbot's supermarket and drinking coffee. They were joined by the tall, thin figure of Henry, a young man in his twenties who loved imparting obscure facts and information to anyone who cared to listen.

'Afternoon ladies,' he said warmly.

'Hi,' said Mary.

'What's an incel?' he inquired.

'Incel?' replied Daphne looking baffled.

'No idea,' said Mary.

'It means involuntary celibate. It mainly involves men who can't get a girlfriend. In a nutshell,' he said clarifying the issue. 'They've formed an online group and have their own website. Many incels tend toward a hatred of women.'

'Wow,' said Mary.

'You're not an incel are you?' Daphne asked cheekily.

'No I'm not,' he replied emphatically. 'But I have a friend and he told me all about it. About their websites and their language.'

'Their language?' inquired Mary.

'Well both of you would be called Stacy's, a regular man with a girlfriend would be called a chad. An attractive bloke would be called a pickup artist. Anyhow he told me that there's an incel working at Talbots,' he said.

'Here?' said Daphne.

'Yeah,' affirmed Henry.

'The deadwood stage is rolling on over the plains!' said Mary, a phrase, taken from the film Calamity Jane, she liked to use when she was determined to find out something.

***

Nick, a young man in his twenties, had worked at Talbot's supermarket for ten years. He worked in the stockroom, unloading and cataloguing deliveries. Small and overweight, his face had a smattering of acne. Nick did his job and kept himself to himself.

Nick spent a lot of time on his computer. He was a member of the online incel community. Nearly every evening he logged into the Men Alone website to converse with his comrades in arms. Some of the people he conversed with in the chatroom were out there and held extreme views. This evening he logged in and began his chat with Keith.

Nick: Saw a few chads today at Talbot's. Smirking, oozing confidence. One was a proper pick-up artist.

Keith: Sick making.

Nick: Also saw a few Stacy's. In love with themselves. Strolling around like they owned the place.

Keith: I'm going to catfish a Stacy.

Nick: Wow.

Keith: I'm going to pretend to be a male model. I can upload a photo of a male model. I'm going to take down a Stacy. Well, it's better than going ER.

Nick: Awesome. I'm going to the gym to try and lose some weight.

Keith: looksmaxing eh. You're now a gymcel.

Nick: Yeah.

Keith: Anyhow got to go. Got to prepare for this catfishing operation.

***

Mary and Daphne were working on the self-service tills; that afternoon Talbot's veered from quite busy to quiet.

'I've got a date tonight,' confided Daphne.

'Wow,' exclaimed Mary.

'Met him on a website,' said Daphne.

'Great!' said Mary, although she didn't quite mean it. As soon as she heard the word website a doubt formed inside her head.

'He's a male model. His name is Geoff. I'm very excited. I'll let you know how I get on,' said Daphne looking as if she'd landed in heaven.

***

Daphne had arranged to meet her date Geoff outside a restaurant called Bennys on the high street. Daphne had provided a photo of herself; there was no mistaking the fact that she was a Goth. They had agreed to have a meal together.

Daphne had arrived five minutes before the agreed time, at six fifty-five. Nervous she felt butterflies in her stomach. Traffic passed, people walked to and fro. An ambulance passed, sirens blazing.

In the distance Daphne saw a small, thin figure approach. He had a gaunt face. As he came close to Daphne, he stared at her. She wondered why he was staring at her. Suddenly he came up to her.

'Daphne?' he exclaimed.

'Yes,' she replied clearly confused. This was not her date; this could not be her date.

'I'm Geoff!' he declared.

She heard the words and for a couple of seconds she could not take it in.

'You're not Geoff!' she replied. She could barely contain her rage. Her mood shifted; she was now on the offensive. 'You're not the man on the website!'

'You thought you were dating a male model!' He started laughing, a glint of malice in his eyes. 'You stupid bitch!'

At this Daphne turned around and started to walk away.

'You've been catfished you whore!' he shouted.

Daphne did not look around. Tears welled up in her eyes. Her tormentor continued to laugh, his laughter morphing into a maniacal cackle.

***

Nick logged on to the chatroom on the Men Alone website.

Nick: How did the catfishing operation go?

Keith: Brilliant. I took down the Stacy.

Nick: How did she react?

Keith: Very angry. She walked away with her tail between her legs. The whole thing gave me life fuel.

Nick: Incels rule!

Keith: Incels rule!

***

The day after the debacle Daphne walked into the staff canteen, purchased a cup of coffee and sat next to her friend Mary. Mary noticed that her friend looked downcast. Just by chance Nick was sitting at an adjacent table.

'How did it go last night? inquired Mary.

'It was a disaster. I was catfished,' she replied.

'Catfished! You mean your date wasn't a male model!

'Exactly. He was a scrawny little shit with a foul mouth. He called me a whore!' declared Daphne visibly upset.

'What! exclaimed Mary.

'Yeah, he verbally abused me, so I walked off. It was all a set up to humiliate me!

'Bastard! exclaimed Mary.

Sitting at a nearby table Nick could not help overhearing this conversation. He listened with disbelief as he realised that the woman who his friend Keith had catfished not only worked at Talbot's but was now sitting at the next table, recounting the disaster. Nick stood up and left the canteen. As he walked out of the canteen Mary stared at him.

'You know Henry was talking about an incel working at Talbot's,' said Mary. Daphne nodded. 'That guy who just walked out…'

'Nick, he works in the stockroom,' said Daphne.

'He's the incel!' declared Mary with certainty.

***

Keith Forbes lived in a high-rise block of flats. In the incel community he was categorised as a Neet; he had zero status as he had no educational qualifications and no job. His world view could only be described as poisonous. He hated the government, benefit officials, psychiatrists and above all women.

Keith suffered from bipolar disorder and as a result was prone to depression. He received ongoing support from a psychiatrist. He described his sessions with his psychiatrist as a duel. His psychiatrist put him on tablets that made him docile.

He idolised Elliot Rogers, an incel who had killed six people in California in 2014. Rogers left behind a manifesto stating that the reason why he was driven to his actions was due to rejection by women. Keith called him the Supreme Gentlemen. Iin the incel community the phrase 'going ER' meant to snap and kill people. This was derived from the killing spree committed by Elliot Rogers. Incels formed an online red pill community. The idea behind this was that the world was ruled by women; men were at the mercy of the whims of women and the identity of a man was either confirmed or destroyed by women. He logged into the chatroom on The Men Alone website.

Keith: Have you seen the video in Sweden. Man walks up to woman in the street and punches her. Clean knockout.

Nick: No, haven't seen it yet. Sounds great. Will check it out.

Keith: Incels rule.

Nick: Incels rule.

***

Peter decided that he would visit the grave of the young man who committed suicide. After all he was the instrument of his death. His name was John Roberts. He was nineteen years of age; he had been studying at college. He suffered from depression. He saw a photo of the young man in the newspaper. The photo gave him a jolt. Peter recalled, for a split second, the young man staring at him, before he jumped in front of the train.

He had an argument with Tina about visiting the gravestone. Quite reasonably she argued that it was pointless; it would only upset him. But Peter was adamant; he just had to do it.

It was a sunny day when he visited the graveyard. It took him twenty minutes to find the grave. It was located next to the grave of a ten-year-old girl, a teddy bear resting against the gravestone of the little girl. Peter dreamily stared at the words on John Roberts' gravestone. Suddenly an elderly woman appeared at the grave, holding some flowers.

'Did you know my son?' she inquired.

Peter momentarily froze. He was face to face with the last person in the world he wanted to see.

'Yes. I knew your son,' he replied, deciding to withhold his real identity.

'He had his whole life ahead of him… I'll never understand it,' she said as she laid the flowers on the grave.

She stood up and they both stared at the grave. Then Peter looked at the old lady.

'Goodbye,' he said to her.

'Goodbye,' and he left her standing over her son's grave.

***

Peter went back to work after a couple of months on sick leave. During this time, he had counselling. He had stopped leaving his wife I Love You notes on the kitchen table. Conversations with his wife were now brief and then hit a dead end. His wife moved into the separate bedroom. Gradually, over time, he drifted apart from his wife. He got drunk more frequently but no amount of alcohol could eliminate the memory of that fateful Monday. His joy for life, his vitality appeared to have deserted him. He stopped going to Elvis Presley conventions. His Elvis Presley outfit lay untouched in the wardrobe.

One day he did some shopping in Talbot's supermarket. On his way out he saw Terry, Talbot's security guard.

'Peter! How are you keeping?' exclaimed Terry.

'Fine thanks. 'He paused. 'I'm back at work now.'

'Great. And Tina?' inquired Terry.

'She's fine.'

'Well… good luck,' said Terry.

'See you later,' said Peter and he took his leave.

***

Mary and Daphne were in the staff canteen when Mary brought up the subject of a video, she saw on You Tube.

'Have you seen that video of that man in Sweden who walks up to the woman and knocks her out?' inquired Mary.

'No,' said Daphne.

'A random act of violence,' said Mary.

'Just random… a stranger attacked a stranger,' said Daphne.

'Totally random,' confirmed Mary. They both noticed Nick sitting at a nearby table. He was sitting close by and could overhear their conversation. Both suspected that he was the incel that Henry referred to. Mary turned to him, drawing him in to the conversation.

'Did you see that video?' inquired Mary.

'Yeah, I saw that video. Terrible.' After talking to Keith, he had checked it out on You Tube. Mary and Daphne looked at each other.

'So you condemn acts of violence against women?' continued Mary.

The atmosphere at the table shifted, a palpable sense of unease and tension suddenly prevailed. Nick stared at Mary. He paused.

'Of course I do!' he replied firmly. He stood up and left the table, leaving behind him an uncomfortable atmosphere.

'He's the incel Henry was talking about,' declared Mary.

'Definitely!' said Daphne.

***

On entering Talbot's supermarket Peter nodded at the security guard Terry. He had drunk a copious amount of alcohol and was struggling, first to retain his balance and second, to remember what he was meant to purchase. He managed to buy the items he had come for and made out for the shortest queue. He joined a queue and standing in front of him was a soldier.

Meanwhile, Terry had watched his friend join the queue. It was clear that his friend was drunk. He decided to go over and talk to him.

Peter looked at the soldier and decided to say something to him.

'Excuse me,' said Peter. The soldier turned around. 'We've got something in common… 'The soldier looked puzzled. 'We both have killed people!'

Sensing trouble Terry intervened and holding Peter's arm motioned him to the self-service section. Peter complied.

'There's nobody in the self-service section Peter,' Terry told him.

Peter paid for his shopping, thanked Terry for his help and then took his leave. He found his way home despite his inebriated state.

***

Nick logged on to the chatroom on the Men Alone website.

Keith: Been to see the shrink. He thinks he's got the key to open my mind. He knows nothing.

Nick: Ok. We live in a red pilled world. But don't do anything stupid.

Keith: I've stopped taking medication prescribed by my shrink. What's the point? Today I went to the coffee house. There was a couple at the next table, a chad and a Stacey. The Stacey had a latte with two shots of espresso.

Nick: Don't tell me. They stared longingly into each other's eyes.

Keith: Exactly. I hated both and I hate the world.

Nick: Go to the gym like me and start toning your body.

Keith: I'm not a gymcel like you. The shrink told me not to sink into a mental torpor.

Nick: What's that?

Keith: That's where life has no meaning, no purpose. You sit at home and vegetate. That's fine for him to say that with his big salary and arrogant attitude. Also, he has a horrible grin.

Nick: How over is it?

Keith: My thoughts are heading in one direction.

Nick: Don't do it.

Keith: I know some incels say lay down and rot. Accept your place in the world. Stay in bed. Watch pornography. Well, I'm not one of them. I'm on the cliff edge looking into the abyss.

Nick: You're not going ER?

Keith: I'm not going to hurt other people. But I'm cutting myself loose.

***

Peter was convinced that he had seen a dead body by the railway line whilst driving his train. He contacted the rail network management and they in turn informed the transport police. Peter was astonished to learn that what he had seen was a nude sunbather.

Two weeks later, pulling out of a station, he once again was stricken with horror. To his left standing close to the railway line was a young man. The young man nonchalantly stared at him for a second. Peter was certain he was going to jump, but this did not happen; his hand was suspended over the emergency brake for a second. Recovering his composure, he alerted the rail network management that there was a young man standing near the railway line.

Peter later learned that young man was detained by transport police. Subsequently the young man had been taken to a mental health unit for observation and assessment.

***

Keith had been here before. His mental health history had prompted the police to take him to the mental health unit. Keith referred to a mental health unit as white space. He was an old hand at navigating his way through the mental health system. The medication he was given had the effect of some huge force pulling him downward toward the earth. He struggled to organise his thoughts. All he had to do was convince the doctors that his brain was devoid of suicidal thoughts.

He had several talks with a psychiatrist. He convinced her that he was feeling lonely and depressed but had no intention of taking his own life. He was prescribed medication and then discharged from the unit after forty-eight hours. When he got home, he went on his computer and logged on to the chatroom on the Men Alone website.

Keith: I've just been locked in white space, shrinks, zombie medication, the works.

Nick: What happened?

Keith: I was detained by the transport police after loitering next to a train line.

Nick: Still feeling low?

Keith: I'm still out there, near the edge.

Nick: I've got to say goodbye. I've got a girlfriend.

Keith: You've ascended. You're becoming a normie. I should have guessed. You were never really an incel. Fuck you. Roll over and die.

Nick did not respond to this abuse. He logged off, never to return to the Men Alone website. Keith fell that bit deeper into his pit of despair.

***

Peter entered Talbot's sheepishly. The last time he was here he was drunk, and his friend Terry had to assist him. He collected his groceries and then went to the self-service section. Peter remembered the young woman from the time he attended the Elvis Presley convention and came into Talbot's for refreshments. Mary, in turn, remembered him. She smiled at him. He was scanning each item of shopping when he noticed a young man pass the self-service section with a small bag of shopping. He recognised him immediately.

'My God!' he exclaimed.

It was the young man who he had seen standing by the railway line. But he had been taken to a mental health unit! Why was he out! Peter took his shopping and left, clearly shaken.

One of the peculiarities of the online incel community was the anonymity. Keith did not know that Nick worked at Talbot's. So, if he had seen him, he would not know him and vice versa. The Men Alone chat room offered a strange mixture of intimacy and anonymity.

At the same time Daphne had re-entered the store and to her amazement had seen the man who had catfished her just leave the store. She approached Mary.

'You'll never guess who I just saw? proclaimed Daphne.

'Who?' said Mary.

'The arsehole who catfished me!' she declared.

When Peter got home, he phoned network rail management. He told his manager he had just seen the young man who he reported for loitering near the railway line.

'The next time… and there will be a next time… he's going to jump in front of a train. I just know it!' emphasised Peter.

After making inquiries the network rail manager told Peter that the young man had been discharged from the mental health unit.

Peter was appalled.

***

The next day Mary and Daphne, after purchasing their coffees from the staff canteen, decided to sit next to Nick who was sitting on his own. Mary decided to engage him in conversation.

'Hi,' she said.

'Hi,' he replied somewhat nervously, after their last exchange.

'Nick, have you heard of the word incel?' Mary inquired.

Nick paused and stared at Mary. How did she know he was involved in the incel community? Anyhow he decided to talk openly about it. He relaxed and began to talk.

'I was involved in the online incel community. But it's a dead end. Incels are eaten up by hatred,' he asserted.

'So you talked with other incels online? Daphne inquired.

'Yeah… about women usually. Horrible things about women. The other day I was having an online chat with a bloke who was thinking of killing himself. 'He paused and looked uncomfortable. Daphne had no idea that they were both talking about the man who had catfished her. 'Look I'm not proud of it. I was wrong. But I'm not a part of that community anymore, I've pulled out. I've ascended,' he declared.

'You've ascended?' Mary looked puzzled.

'In the incel community you've ascended when you get a girlfriend. I've now got a girlfriend. I've moved on. 'Nick said this with a look of tranquillity. Mary smiled at Daphne.

***

Peter had just finished his shift, when he bumped into one of his colleagues, Fred. Fred had been on the job now for five years. Chirpy and cheerful he was popular with his colleagues.

'I'm going your way Peter, jump in the driver's carriage with me, I'll drop you off,' said Fred.

'Ok,' replied Peter.

'How's things anyway… I know you had that suicide some months back,' inquired Fred.

'I'm fine… driving ok now,' replied Peter.

Fred started the train and it moved forward slowly. Fred was a confident driver. The train moved clear of the railway station. Then suddenly Peter and Fred saw a young man standing on the left, near the railway line. In a flash Peter knew what was going to happen.

'Jesus!' exclaimed Fred.

The young man jumped in front of the train. Fred hit the emergency brakes. He was shaking and his skin was pale. When the train stopped, Peter told Fred to alert the rail network manager. He would go out and see what happened to the young man, although there could only be one outcome. Peter walked back along the railway line until he came upon the human remains of the young man, including his severed head. The dead young man was the same man Peter had reported to the rail network.

'This time you jumped,' he said to himself.

***

The next day Peter entered Talbot's supermarket for groceries. Terry, the security guard was talking to his colleague Mary. They were looking at the newspaper, at the photo of the man who had hurled himself in front of a train. Terry looked up and saw Peter. When Peter saw him looking at the photo he interjected.

'I saw him here yesterday…'

'You're right… he was here,' said Terry suddenly remembering.

'I warned them…' emphasised Peter.

Daphne joined her friend Mary and looked at the photo in the newspaper. She looked astonished. Mary glanced at her friend and noticed her change in expression.

'What's the matter?' inquired Mary.

'That's my date from hell, real name Keith, the guy who catfished me!'

***

After taking some time off Peter returned to work. Slowing down, the train moved into the station, near the location where the student threw himself in front of Peter's train. Peter felt queasy when he saw flowers tied to the railings. The flowers were a gesture of remembrance for bereaved relatives but were a distressing reminder to the train driver that they were involved in a fatal event.

Really bloody sad.
but good.

The Librarian

In the beginning there was Jason and the Argonauts, that is according to the world as viewed by David Brooks. The film of this ancient story filled his boyish imagination with wonder and awe. He would learn that sometimes the legend becomes fact.

***

'Don't accept your fate! You must fight. They are coming!'

The elderly man who made this statement had staring eyes and a shambolic appearance. After making his bizarre statement to the two shop assistants the man turned and walked away. Mary and Daphne watched the man walk away and then looked at each other in bemusement. They were working on the self-service till at Talbot's supermarket. High ceilings, row upon row of stacked shelves and omnipresent signs, Talbot's was one of the largest supermarkets in south-east London.

'What was that about?' asked Mary.

'No idea. I've seen him before. Looks like a mad professor. I think that man needs help,' said Daphne.

***

David Brooks always had an active, some would say a wild imagination. Coming home one day on the school bus he passed Shooters Hill. Looking out of the bus on the top deck, he saw a scaffold, in the shape of an L and saw a man hanging from the scaffold. In the nineteenth century Shooters Hill was a place where criminals were hanged. Looking around the bus it was clear that nobody else saw the corpse hanging from the scaffold. He got off the bus to see the hanging man, but when he got to the junction in the road the hanging man had vanished. When he went home and told his mother she told him to stop telling tales and to concentrate on his school studies.

His mother Beryl, like any doting mother, worried about her son. She worked as a shop assistant in Talbot's supermarket. She was so concerned about his flights of fancy that she considered consulting a doctor. Rejecting this she hoped that it was just a passing phase.

Travelling on the bus along New Cross road he saw a huge hole in the road. Inside the hole was an upturned bus, its rear end high in the air. During the second world war this area had been attacked by V2 rockets. David closed his eyes and opened them again. The upturned bus was gone. David's imagination was a time tunnel that afforded him graphic images of the past. He did not tell his mother about this disturbing image.

***

The class on Greek mythology turned out to be more interesting than David thought. The teacher talked about Jason and the Argonauts. How Jason's uncle Pelias kills Jason's father the Greek king of lolkos and takes his throne. How Jason, to restore his rightful place on the throne, was given a task to complete. He had to capture the golden fleece. In doing so he had to overcome several obstacles. He assembled a team of Argonauts, each with a special skill or quality. Jason eventually completes his quest.

During the talk by the teacher David asked a question.

'Why was the old man Phineas blinded?'

'Good question. Phineas was blinded by Zeus as punishment because he misused his powers of prophecy.'

A couple of weeks after the class he watched the film Jason and the Argonauts on television. He was mesmerised and captivated. Jason's heroic bravery was tested to the limit. The film was full of unforgettable images. The bronze giant Talos who guarded Crete against pirates. Jason discovered his weakness, in his heel and by exploiting this he killed Talos. The demonic harpies, half human, half bird who tormented Phineas. Finally, Jason confronted the nine headed hydra, that protected the golden fleece. Jason killed the hydra, but it came back to haunt Jason. The hydra's teeth were transformed into demonic skeletons armed with sword and shields. Jason manages to escape their demonic energy with his life.

***

David was at home with his mother Beryl in the kitchen, eating their tea. The day before Beryl, a bubbly woman in her early forties had introduced her son to her new suitor Roger. Divorced for five years, she had finally decided to look for love. She was keen to know what David thought of her new suitor.

'What did you think of Roger?' she asked nervously.

'He's a giant,' said David brusquely.

'Well he's a body builder. He runs a gym in the high street. He keeps himself in shape,' said Beryl.

'He looks like Talos,' declared David to his mystified mother.

'Who's Talos? she asked.

'Talos was the bronze giant who protected the island of Crete from pirates in Greek myth. Talos mistook Jason and the argonauts for pirates and Jason killed Talos,' said David.

'Oh,' said Beryl looking baffled. 'But you do like him don't you? I mean he's nice, isn't he?

'He's okay,' said David half-heartedly.

David didn't like or trust Roger. David had recently watched a documentary about lightning and discovered that the chances of a person being hit by a bolt of lightning were five hundred thousand to one. So, Roger was unlikely to be hit by a bolt of lightning.

Also, it was unlikely, thought David, that Roger would be covered in radioactive material, in a freak accident, and then consequently all his bodily organs begin to shrink. This is what happened in one of David's favorite sci-fi films, The Incredible Shrinking Man, where a sinister mist covers the central character whilst he is sunbathing on a boat.

He decided to make enquiries about the gym that Roger ran.

***

David watched the film The Matrix at home entranced. His mother brought him a cup of tea. She sat down on the settee near him.

'What a great film!' he declared.

'So what is the Matrix then?'

'Well the Matrix is a form of virtual reality. Everything in the matrix, scenes and objects are created by a computer.'

'So the Matrix is not real?'

'Well to the people in the Matrix it is real. I mean look at Talbot's supermarket. Is that real or is it part of the Matrix?'

'Now David, I can assure you that Talbot's supermarket is very real. I tell you what, you stick to the Matrix and I'll stick to old progammes on TV like Randall and Hopkirk Deceased. My imagination is still alive. It's not deceased!' old show

***

At school a few days later, David was in the dining room eating his sandwiches for lunch and scanning the texts on his smartphone. He was joined at his table by two other schoolboys, Terry and Warren. Both were wiry and liked talking about films.

'Did you see the Matrix last night on TV?' asked Terry.

Both David and Warren nodded their heads as they were fans of the film. This, after all, was the film where the fantastic was made flesh. Terry continued. 'I love that scene where Neo played by Keanu Reeves jumps from one building to another building. Awesome man!'

'Yeah! That's a great scene,' gasped Warren.

'Have you seen Andy Bishop today?' asked Terry.

'No,' said David munching on his sandwich.

Terry suddenly looked furtive and looked around the room, as if he was to impart some secret. David and Warren moved closer to Terry.

'He's into drugs!' he declared.

'He'll mess up his body man,' declared Warren.

'I've heard that he gets his drugs from the gym on the high street!' said Terry.

David remained silent, slowly absorbing this information. Could Roger be a drug dealer?

***

David went to the local library to seek out more information about Jason and the Argonauts. It was a small library. All those words and stories trapped in those books, he thought to himself, waiting to be liberated by the reader. In the far corner sat a bespectacled man sitting behind a desk. David approached him and asked if he had any books on the subject. The man smiled and walked to a bookshelf. He had the soothing voice and manner of a doctor.

'A very interesting subject, Greek mythology. In this world of science and technology we forget that there is a world beyond understanding, of infinite possibility. A world where skeletons rise from the earth and turn into demons!'

David warmed to the subject and nodded his head. The librarian picked up a book and handed it to him.

'Great, thanks,' said David.

'This has a section on Jason and the Argonauts. 'He paused. 'Do you believe in magic?'

'Yes, I do.'

'Do you attend St. Thomas the Apostle secondary school by any chance?'

'Yeah. That's my school.'

'I'm going there next Tuesday to help sort out the library catalogue database.'

The librarian processed his book and David took his leave. The librarian made a deep impression on him. He was like a figure of infinite wisdom out of a film about supernatural forces.

***

The huge painting of Jesus Christ carrying the cross that overlooked the main stairway of St. Thomas Apostle school always captured David's eye. It was tragic and majestic at the same time. He was walking past the stairway, to the concourse that led to the corridor of the ground floor. Students and teachers moved along the corridor in both directions. When he entered the corridor, he saw the librarian at the other end of the corridor walking toward him. At one point he walked past a fire alarm glass panel on the wall. As he got near David he smiled.

'Hello Mr. Brooks.'

'Hello.'

Within seconds of passing the fire alarm glass panel the glass shattered, as if smashed by an invisible force. Then the fire alarm was activated, creating a wave of noise that assaulted the ears. David stopped and stared at the shattered glass on the ground. Then everyone in the corridor, including David and the librarian made their way to the nearest exit. David instructed the librarian to go to the assembly point, in the playground.

In the playground David began to talk to the librarian.

'I don't understand how that glass panel shattered? Nobody was near it.'

The librarian looked at David and smiled as if he possessed some secret knowledge that he did not want to impart.

***

In David's mind one word summed up his mother: innocent. She could be vague and distracted, she loved animals and watching animal rescue programmes. She always cried when she saw Judy Garland sing Over the Rainbow when the film The Wizard of Oz was shown on TV. But she was incapable of seeing through Roger. How was it possible that a lovely woman like his mother could fall in love with a horrible man like Roger?

So, David decided to visit Gym World, the place of Rogers' business. His first impression of Roger was a man bestowed with an exceptional physique. He was well over six feet, his broad shoulders accompanied with a small waist. His body mass was an accumulation of muscle as opposed to fat. Hence David's description of him as Talos. In conversation he was polite but terse. It was clear that he did not want to give too much away.

David entered Gym World on the pretext of doing some exercise to build a muscular frame. The front of the building was splashed with a garish yellow sign that read Gym World. He paid a small fee at reception and then entered an area that contained an assortment of machinery. Sweating men and women, strained expressions on their faces, were working out. Most of them had muscular frames. Like Jason in Greek mythology, they were on their personal quest, for their own version of the golden fleece, the perfect body. This was a place where human muscle triumphed over human fat. David decided to work on the exercise bicycle. After a while he worked up a decent sweat. All the time David was keeping an eye out for Roger.

In the distance David caught sight of Roger lifting weights. Roger stood up and used a towel to remove the sweat from his body. He then picked up his mobile phone and took a selfie. David's view of him as a preening narcissist was confirmed. Some young men approached and began to talk to him. The conversation appeared to become heated. Then Roger broke away. Seeing David, he approached him smiling.

'Well, well! Working up a good sweat David.'

'Yeah. But I'm getting tired.'

'Well I'll leave you to it. Remember David you've got to work past the pain. Your body is a temple. You've got to look after it. I'm visiting your mum tomorrow night so I'll be seeing you.'

As Roger walked away David's suspicion of him intensified.

***

During his wrestling career Mike adopted the name The Tornado. People at Talbot's were aware of his colorful past. Of Nigerian origin, Mike was stocky with broad shoulders and muscled biceps. A man with gentle smile he was well liked at Talbot's and had worked as a security guard there for five years. As an ex-wrestler he could still deploy several moves when necessary, such as a chokeslam or a half nelson.

David entered Talbot's and greeted Mike, an acquaintance of his mothers.'

'Hi Mike!'

'Hi David! Your mum is in the staff room, she'll be out in a few minutes.'

'Thanks Mike.'

Looking at Mike David thought that he would make an ideal Argonaut.

***

David's bedroom walls were splashed with movie posters, one depicting a giant tarantula, another depicting a flying saucer crashing into government buildings in Washington and another of a shark's fin protruding from the water. But his favourite poster was of Jason in combat with the skeleton soldiers from the film. That evening, at home in his bedroom David immersed himself in a video game, Grand Theft Auto. The aerial view of the cityscape, as portrayed by the game, was enthralling. In this game the scenario was a bank robbery. David took on the role of the police officer dispatched to deal with the bank robber. The bank robber, hooded and sinister, was armed. David was adept at deploying the handset attached to the video game and in the final confrontation he shot and killed the bank robber. One day, he thought to himself, he might be a hero in the real world.

***

The following day at school David attended an English literature class. During the first term the class covered the Gothic novel Premature Burial by Edgar Allen Poe. The subject of the novel appealed to David's dark imagination. A British aristocrat has a morbid fear of being buried alive. His fear is eventually realised. A horrible thought did cross David's mind whilst reading this story: Roger being buried alive. But David conceded that although Roger was odious, he did not deserve this cruel fate.

The young teacher, just out of college was enthusiastic and fluent in her subject. The subject was Shakespeare. The class was attentive. The teacher asked students to think of a famous Shakespearean quote.

'By the pricking of my thumbs something wicked this way comes,' offered a student.

'Good.'

'There are more things in heaven and earth than are dreamt of in your philosophy,' offered another student.

'Excellent!' exclaimed the teacher. 'Then she looked at David. 'David have you got a quote?'

'Space the final frontier, these are the voyages of the starship Enterprise, its five-year mission to explore strange new worlds, to seek out new civilizations, to boldly go where no man has gone before!'

The class burst into laughter. The teacher smiled.

'Well it's not Shakespeare but I'll admit that Star Trek does have cultural value. Thank you, David.'

That evening David visited the gym again, doing some exercise on a bike. When he left, he noticed a group of men congregating around the rear exit door. Observing them from a distance he saw money and small packets change hands. At the center of the group was Roger.

***

One Saturday David invited his best friend, Warren, to his house to watch the film Jason and the Argonauts. Excitable and friendly Warren was popular at school. Warren loved the film and marveled at the special effects. His favourite scene was the skeleton fight with Jason and the Argonauts, a sentiment shared by David. They were alone in the house.

'Do you want a new experience?' inquired Warren.

'What do you mean?' said David.

'I can talk to Walter White at Gym World and get some stuff. You know Walter White from Breaking Bad, the guy who becomes a drug dealer.'

'So there's a Walter White character at Gym World who sells drugs?'

'Sure. That's not his real name… but that's what he calls himself. Big guy works out. Gigantic biceps, massive shoulders. Well? Are you up for it?'

'Yeah, sure.'

'I'll get the stuff tomorrow. You know Gary… the brainbox?'

'Yeah.'

'Well I'll go with him. He gets his stuff from Walter White. I'll meet you tomorrow just after lunch, at two o'clock. At the entrance to Banbury maze.'

'Ok.'

***

David and Warren enjoyed the visual beauty of Eden maze and liked to wander around the maze. A dizzying network of paths the maze rendered the human mind disorientated and confused. Warren arrived promptly at two o'clock, in an excitable frame of mind.

'I've got them!' Warren declared.

'Great! Let's take a walk.'

They entered the maze and David handed Warren a can of soft drink. They followed the path, turning left and right until they came to a bench. They sat down. Warren took out a small packet and removed a tablet and put it in his mouth, followed by a swig of the soft drink. He removed another tablet from the packet and gave it to David, who did the same as Warren. Then they both sat back and looked up at the sky.

'You know that Walter White bloke, he reminds me of Talos in Jason and the Argonauts!' said Warren.

'I know exactly what you mean,' agreed David.

'How do you feel?' asked Warren.

'A bit strange,' said David. After a few minutes he felt buzzing with energy. 'I tell you what I feel great!'

'Let's get out of here,' said Warren.

They stood up and moved through the maze swiftly searching for the exit. Suddenly David was confronted by an unearthly vision, that blocked his way through the maze. A skeleton with a sword and a shield! He stopped dead in his tracks.

'Oh my God! Let's get out the other way,' David exclaimed.

'What's the matter?' said Warren.

David turned around and took another route out of the maze, moving swiftly.

'Didn't you see the skeleton?'

At this Warren laughed. On leaving the maze Warren turned to

David.

'That's one of the effects of the drug. Makes you see things that don't exist!' exclaimed Warren.

***

David's mother had asked him to post a letter. He walked slowly to the letterbox, about a quarter of a mile away. He was a couple of yards from the letterbox when somebody behind him called his name.

'Mr. Brooks! Don't post the letter!'

David stopped, turned around and saw the man from the library. He was confused. Then suddenly a car swerved off the main road and crashed into the letterbox. The car was mangled, and the driver bloodied but still alive. David turned around, but the librarian had vanished. He realised that if the librarian had not stopped him from posting the letter he would have been hit by the car.

***

David and Warren were regulars at The Café. Sipping coffee and eating their burgers and chips David recounted his experience posting the letter.

'This librarian appeared out of nowhere and told me not to post the letter. I was right near the letterbox. Then a car crashed into the letterbox!'

'He has the gift of prophecy!'

'You're right. He does have the gift of prophecy.'

At that moment a group of teenagers, two boys and a girl, entered the café and sat down. Unruly and loud they ordered their food. Nearby a blind man was eating a sandwich. They looked at the blind man and laughed. David and Warren sensed trouble and had stopped talking. Tariq, the owner of the café served them their food. They devoured their food, then the tall teenager walked over to the blind man, picked up a sandwich from his plate and ate it. The blind man was silent; he knew someone had removed something from his plate. He was silent in his humiliation. The only sound that could be heard in the cafe was the laughter from the wild trio. Tariq looked on, too scared to intervene. Laughing, the trio paid for their meal then left.

Tariq kindly replaced the sandwich for the blind man.

'Those three are just like the harpies in Jason and the Argonauts…' said David.

'How do you mean?'

'The blind man Phineas who is tormented by the harpies. Remember?'

'Of course. Listen, I've seen them at Gym World. They get their drugs from there.'

'Yeah, they're harpies alright. Half bird and half human all they do is destroy things. One day they'll get their comeuppance, just like in Jason and the Argonauts!'

***

Henry was holding forth in Talbot's café about terrorist attacks on public places. Henry often adopted the manner of a teacher and liked the sound of his own voice. Mary, Daphne and Beryl listened patiently.

'Listen if a terrorist attacks Talbot's then we have two options. First, find the nearest exit and flee. An honorable thing to do, given the immediate prospect of death. Second, we can retreat and fight,' he declared.

'How do you mean?' asked Daphne.

'Well if you can get to the alcohol section of Talbot's you've got a selection of bottles of wine, whiskey, vodka. In other words, you have a supply of weapons that can be directed against the terrorist!'

'Of course!' said Beryl.

***

David was at home with his mother, eating their evening meal. He knew that later Roger was taking his mother out for a meal.

'Does Roger ever talk about his business dealings at Gym World?' asked David tentatively.

'No David. 'Beryl was clearly annoyed by the question.

'You know that there's drug dealing going on at Gym World,' declared David.

Beryl put down her knife and fork, clearly exasperated.

'I don't believe it!' she asserted.

'It's true. A friend of mine at school told me. Honest mum.'

'Well even if it is true it's got nothing to do with Roger.'

This statement concluded the conversation. David took his plate to the kitchen then went to his bedroom.

***

At the weekend David and his friend Warren liked to surf the DLR (the Docklands Light Railway). When David used the phrase surf the DLR he meant the sane version of this practice, namely remaining inside the train as opposed to the insane version where thrill seekers surfed on the top of the train. The DLR was the train system that traversed London. Elevated on concrete pillars the train swerved, left and right around London. David usually got on at Greenwich and enjoyed the swerving motion of the train until it reached what David called the emerald city, that is the giant towers of Canary Wharf. He called Canary Wharf the emerald city after seeing the film The Wizard of Oz.

David was returning from Canary Wharf one Saturday when he saw the librarian on the DLR. He now knew who the librarian resembled. The previous week he had watched an old film on TV called Dracula. The librarian looked like Van Helsing, the man who's mission in life was to kill Dracula. The librarian had the same sunken in face and the same old-world courtesy as the actor who played Van Helsing, Peter Cushing.

Two young men, brawny and surly, were sitting near the librarian. They got up together and faced the librarian menacingly. The atmosphere on the train suddenly changed.

'Hand over your money grandad!' said the taller man.

The librarian looked at the two men; he appeared calm and unafraid. He stood up and moved his right arm with a sweeping motion. To David's amazement the tall man was lifted off the floor and hurled against the train window by some invisible force. The librarian then delivered another sweeping motion of his right arm, and the smaller man was lifted off his feet and propelled against the same window, with the effect that both were rendered unconscious. The librarian then calmly walked away. On getting off the train he noticed David.

'Your library book is due to be returned.'

'Ok,' said an incredulous David.

David immediately thought of the film Star Wars. The librarian wasn't like Van Helsing in Dracula; he was like Obi-Wan Kenobi in Star Wars. He was able to harness the force.

***

The following week at school the teacher covered the subject of Nostradamus, the famous prophet. The teacher was sceptical about his prophecies, as were all the students, including David. The first prophecy included the dropping of the nuclear bombs on Hiroshima and Nagasaki. 'Within two cities there will be scourges the like of which was never seen' wrote Nostradamus. The second prophecy concerned the assassination of President Kennedy. 'From on high evil will fall on the great man. A dead innocent will be accused of the deed. 'The second part of the prophecy, a clear reference to Lee Harvey Oswald, struck many of the students as eerie. The third prophecy concerned the rise of Hitler. 'A young child will be born of poor people. He will by his tongue seduce a great troop. 'Again students were not totally convinced by the prophecy.

However, David could not explain how the librarian seemed to know that the car was going to crash into the letterbox.

***

David was at Gym World working out on the exercise bicycle when he suddenly saw two members of staff rush to the door leading to the rear of the building. A scuffle had broken out at the rear of building between some men. He learned that a man was injured and had to go to hospital.

The next day at school in the dining room David told his friend Warren about the incident at Gym World.

'It's a turf war between drug dealers,' declared Warren. 'That's what I heard. This new dealer has arrived on the scene.'

'Do you think it involves this Walter White character you were talking about?'

'Definitely.'

***

That evening, eating dinner with his mother, she spoke about her beau Roger. She was clearly worried.

'Roger said that he's going to stop working out for a while. He's got this condition called Achillies' tendonitis.'

'What's that?'

'Well he told me that's where you have pain and stiffness around your lower leg.'

'You mean around his heel?'

'Yeah. He said it's been getting worse and worse.'

'Just like Talos!'

'Pardon?'

'Nothing.'

David continued to eat his meal. He reflected that Roger, just like Talos in Greek mythology, had a physical weakness around his lower leg.

***

David and Warren were at the The café eating burgers and chips, the smell of fried food wafting through the café. The blind man was there quietly eating his meal when in walked Mike, the security guard from Talbot's. He smiled at David, and they exchanged greetings. He ordered his meal and sipped a cup of coffee in the meantime.

Then the troublesome trio entered the café. They sat down laughing and joking and ordered their meal. Mike watched them carefully. They drank their soft drinks, staring at the blind man. The blind man was aware of the presence of his tormentors and seemed tense. The young man amongst the trio got up and approached his table. Laughing, with an unbearable mocking laugh, he suddenly grabbed the man's burger from his plate and began to eat it in front of him.

Mike, David and Warren watched this scene play out. David and Warren were about to witness the fury and rage that this incident evoked in Mike, who wasn't described once as the tornado for nothing. The ensuing tornado took the harpies by surprise. Mike suddenly stood up.

'Put that back!' he exclaimed.

The belligerent teenager turned around and looked at Mike. The other scruffy male teenager and his female friend stood up threateningly from their table, suddenly aware that they were being challenged.

'Fuck you!' mouthed the tall teenager.

Suddenly Mike sprang into action. He advanced at speed at his tall foe and delivered a fierce upper cut that felled his opponent. The girl screamed and charged him, whereupon he slammed her face on the table. Mike turned to the remaining male teenager who charged him. But Mike saw this move coming and got him in a headlock and then delivered a chokeslam that knocked out his opponent. This meant that, after getting him in a headlock, jumping in the air, with his arm wrapped around the teenagers' head and landing on the floor backward.

Tariq, David and Warren watched this violent spectacle in silence. The three teenagers, barely conscious were picked up off the floor by a victorious Mike, one by one and marched to the café door. When he turned around Tariq addressed him.

'Your meal is on the house.'

'You'd make a great Argonaut,' declared David.

A dazed Mike looked mystified by this last comment. The blind man was given another meal by Tariq. David and Warren looked at each other and smiled. As far as David was concerned the harpies were vanquished by a brave Argonaut and Phineas had been liberated.

***

David paid a visit to his local library to return his book. The librarian was there, sitting behind his desk, inscrutable and polite. He now felt he had a relationship with the librarian. It was clear that the librarian possessed some strange power.

'Did you enjoy the book?'

'Yes. Very much.'

'As I told you the last time I saw you, there is a world beyond the everyday.'

'How did you know that car was going to crash into that post-box?'

'Magic. I can tell that you are interested in magic.'

He stood up to return the book to its place on the bookshelf. David followed him.

'You're like Nostradamus!'

'I take that as a compliment.'

'I sometimes see things out of the past.'

'Your imagination is tuned in to the past. Interesting. I thought that maybe you had special qualities. You know David that there's a world out there beyond the realm of science. 'He turned around and looked at David. 'Soon you will be tested. I can give you something very precious that will help you.'

He walked back to his desk and opened a drawer. He picked up a small pouch.

'Remember the skeleton soldiers summoned by the king in the story of Jason and the Argonauts.'

'Sure. The skeleton soldiers. Fantastic man!'

'Well this pouch contains the hydra's teeth. My grandfather in Greece handed them down to my father and my father handed them down to me.'

'You mean the hydra's teeth that morphed into the skeleton soldiers?'

'Exactly. One day you will find yourself in peril. When that day comes you will have an advantage, the hydra's teeth. I will give you this pouch. Look after it carefully. When the time comes you can summon the skeleton soldiers, the children of the night. They can be summoned to protect you from the forces of evil. Remember this. Throw the teeth on earth and then repeat the following incantation. Rise up you dead, slain of the hydra. You can then direct them to destroy the evildoers, whoever they are.'

The librarian handed the pouch to David.

'Are you serious?'

'One day you will find out I'm speaking the truth.'

***

Warren told David that he saw Walter White the previous day near a block of flats. He was removing plastic bags from the rear of his car.

'Plastic bags?' asked David.

'Yeah. Full of money I reckon. He is a drug dealer. And he was limping,' said Warren.

'Walter White is my mum's partner! And his name is Roger,' said David.

'What! He's a drug dealer man!' stated Warren.

'I've tried to tell my mum. She won't listen,' said David with resignation.

'Well there's some nasty characters trying to take over his patch. He'd better watch out,' opined Warren.

***

David visited his mother at Talbot's supermarket. On entering the supermarket, he noticed a change to the layout. On the right-hand side, the company had added a small rectangular area consisting of flowers and some soil. David had been enthralled by his conversation with the librarian and removed the pouch from his pocket. He had checked the contents of the pouch: it contained a collection of large teeth. What would happen if he threw the hydra's teeth on the soil around the flowers and then recited the incantation?

He stopped near the bed of flowers and looked around. Nobody was looking at him. Then he repeated the incantation.

'Rise up you dead, slain of the hydra. Destroy the evildoers!'

However, he did not throw the hydra's teeth on the flower bed. But he did enjoy reciting the incantation.

***

At home with his mother, they were sitting at the dining room table, eating their tea. His mother had cooked a delicious chicken curry.

'Do you believe in magic mum? Like the supernatural?'

'Magic? No, not really.'

'The other day, something happened to me. And it can't really be explained.'

Beryl's face became animated; she looked concerned.

'What happened?'

'Remember you asked me to post that letter? Well as I approached the letterbox a man stopped me and told me to wait. Then a car lost control and crashed into the letterbox. If I hadn't been stopped by that man that car would have hit me.'

'My God!'

'The man who stopped me is the librarian. He works at the library where I get my books. He's like Obi-Wan Kenobi in Star Wars. He can harness the force.'

'Well, why don't you harness the force after this meal and do your homework!'

***

The next time David saw Roger at Gym World he was walking into his office, limping. Roger said hello to David, but he looked tense. The cocky swagger had disappeared. Warren's warning of an impending turf battle between two drug gangs proved prescient.

A rival drug gang took advantage of Rogers' weakness and staged a brutal attack as he left Gym World one evening. He was surrounded by four men wielding baseball bats. He was savagely beaten, the result being that his left leg was broken.

Beryl visited Roger in hospital, weeping. She spent nearly the whole day at the hospital, supporting Roger. That evening she returned home and made the evening meal for herself and David.

She was visibly upset.

'How's he doing?' asked David.

'Well his leg is broken. He has bruises on his face, arms and chest. They could have killed him! And the police keep asking him questions. I don't understand why he was attacked?'

'He'll get better mum.'

David reflected that his mother was still ignorant of the fact that her beau was a drug dealer; and he was certainly not going to tell her. He also reflected that like Talos Roger's downfall was a weakness related to his feet.

***

The next day a visibly upset Beryl told David that things had gone from bad to worse: Roger had been arrested by the police on suspicion of selling illegal drugs. Beryl looked stunned. She told David that the relationship was now over. David was relieved but did not admit his emotions to his mother.

The following day at school David's friend Warren sat next to him in a noisy dining room.

'Have you heard? Walter White got done over by a drug gang.'

'Yeah. I know. My mum visited him in hospital. He's got a broken leg.'

'Does she know he's a drug dealer?'

'Yeah! He's been arrested by the police for selling illegal drugs. My mum has ended the relationship finally. So, all's well that ends well!'

There was a pause as they drank their coffee. David continued, changing the subject.

'Listen. I saw the librarian and he gave me a pouch containing some magical objects!'

'What do you mean?'

'You do believe in magic don't you?'

'Of course.'

'You know in Jason and the Argonauts, the skeleton soldiers that are created by the hydra's teeth?'

'Sure.'

'Well the librarian has got magical powers. He's from Greece. He was given the hydra's teeth by his dad. He gave the hydra's teeth to me in a pouch. When I'm in situation of peril I'm to throw the teeth on earth and then recite the incantation.'

'Wow! So, you can summon demon skeletons!'

'Yeah!'

'So, what's the incantation?'

'Rise up you dead, slain of the hydra's teeth!'

'Let's see them!'

'Sorry, I'm not showing them to anyone. I just know that they really are the hydra's teeth. The librarian called the skeleton soldiers the children of the night. One day I'll need them!'

***

A dingy flat in south-east London. The sunlight poured in from a window. Three young men were standing next to a table, staring at the table. All three were of athletic build. Bristling with energy, these men were on a mission. They seemed to be in some sort of trance. On the table there were six knifes and duct tape. Each of the men picked up a knife and turned toward each other. Each of the men stretched out their arms, holding a knife to the same central point. They looked at each other, eyes blazing with hatred. Then in unison, their brains on the same wavelength, they uttered the same word.

'Death!'

***

Henry was walking through Talbot's supermarket after completing some accounts work in the office. He stopped to talk to Beryl who was working on the self-service tills. Beryl was still upset by the attack on Roger, but she soldiered on and came to work. Talbot's was busy, music was playing in the background. She was authorising the purchase of alcohol for a man, making the necessary entry on the cash screen.

'Hi Beryl.'

'Hi Henry.'

'How's David?'

'Fine thanks.'

'I just had a word with big Mike. I was at St Pancras station yesterday and I noticed the police were carrying arms. I saw two officers carrying a machine gun! You know what that means?'

'No. What does it mean?'

'The terrorist threat level has been upgraded. So, everybody needs to be vigilant.'

'Ok.'

Henry walked off and Beryl returned to her work, thinking to herself that Henry was exaggerating the risk.

***

It was a quiet afternoon at Talbot's supermarket. Footfall was quite low, staff replenished the shelves, music floated across the supermarket. Kylie Minogue's The Locomotion filled the air. Beryl was working on the self-service tills; big Mike was on duty as security near the entrance. Mike greeted David when he entered the supermarket. David had come to the store to buy some groceries. As he passed the self-service tills he waved to his mother; she reciprocated. He noticed a yellow sign in the frozen meat section, caused by a spillage of milk. He then purchased some bread and milk.

Outside in the car park nobody took much notice of the three men getting out of a car. Their images would be recorded by CCTV. They moved slowly toward the entrance. As they entered the outer foyer area Mike noticed them. He was suddenly aware that each man seemed to be carrying an object, in each hand. Then, to his horror, he saw one of the men move his arm violently, and a man standing nearby, fell to the ground. A woman nearby screamed and fled away from the supermarket. Struggling to comprehend the situation Mike realised that he had just witnessed a violent attack.

The screaming alerted people inside the store that something dramatic and terrible was unfolding. Beryl looked toward the entrance. David was just about to scan his items in the self-service area when he too stopped and looked toward the entrance.

Mike, sensing extreme danger, pressed a button to close the automatic entrance doors. The three men (clearly armed) advanced toward the entrance door. Mike, previously seated, was now on his feet. One of the men grabbed the door before it closed.

David realised that the moment of peril that the librarian had talked about had arrived. He knew what he had to do next. He looked at his mother, trying to overcome his panic.

'Mum. Get out! Use the rear exit.'

She ran to the rear exit. He felt in his pocket for the pouch and ran to the small garden area near the entrance. There was a small desk, for the sale of newspapers and tobacco nearby, and David ran behind it when he saw the three men, all armed, get past the door. Mike bravely grabbed one of the men and body slammed him to the floor. But the second man plunged his knife into Mike's back; Mike stumbled and then fell to the floor. David watched this grim sight from behind the desk thinking that Mike fought like a brave Argonaut. The three men did not see him.

Meanwhile panic and screaming had erupted in the store, people running to the rear of the building. The three men, all armed, had moved to the interior of the building, like unstoppable demons. David stood up, moved to the small garden area and pulled out a pouch from his pocket. He emptied the contents of the pouch on to the garden soil and then began to recite the following words.

'Rise up you dead, you slain of the hydra's teeth.'

Suddenly the soil moved. Then three skeletons emerged from the soil, a chilling sight. Each skeleton was armed with a sword and a shield. David could hardly believe his eyes. He continued.

'Kill, kill the evildoers!'

Initially erect the upper and lower half of the skeletons suddenly bent forward and they moved with demonic speed in pursuit of the armed men. One of the armed men had cornered a shopper in the alcohol section. The shopper had bravely fought off his attacker by throwing bottles of wine at the deranged man. One of the bottles had struck the armed man and hurt him. Suddenly he was confronted, to his amazement, by a skeleton, armed with a sword and a shield. The skeleton advanced toward the armed man and they engaged in combat. The skeleton parried a knife thrust with his shield and then thrust his sword into the chest of the armed man. He fell, struggling to breathe until he died.

The second skeleton headed toward the fruit and vegetable section where the second armed man was chasing a terrified young woman. When the armed man saw the skeleton, he stopped in his tracks immediately. Now the tables were turned. The armed man recovered his composure and attacked the skeleton. A fierce fight ensued, apples and bananas were thrust in the air after being struck by the young man when he missed the skeleton. At one point he was pushed into a shelf of vegetables. He lost his balance and was then killed by the skeleton.

The third armed man was hunting down a young man in the frozen meat section, but he was thwarted by the spillage near the yellow sign. Advancing toward the young man he slipped when he came to the spillage near the yellow sign. This allowed the young man to escape. When the armed man got to his feet he turned around and was confronted by a skeleton, armed with a sword. Staring in disbelief, the armed man forgot to defend himself and was attacked with a thrust to the chest. He fell to the floor.

David could no longer hear shouting and screaming so he got up from behind the desk. Staff and customers were walking around dazed. In the frozen meat section, he saw the dead body of the armed young man on the floor. Next to him was a heap of bones, a sword and shield. The demonic skeletons had disappeared as quickly as they appeared. The librarian was right: magic really does exist.

Robin Hood

'Do you really know your neighbour?' asked Harry Dobbs, in between sipping his tea, in the canteen of Talbot's supermarket.

Harry Dobbs was a young man with a fearsome physical appearance. Stocky and muscular he had a pock-marked face and a nervous, mobile face. A live wire he gave off nervous energy. He seemed to be plugged into the National Grid. He posed the question to the small group of Talbot's employees who were on their break. He was flanked by his friend Terry Bishop, a large man who worked in the warehouse and looked perpetually worried. Sitting opposite Harry Dobbs were Mary and Daphne, two young store assistants. Daphne was marked out by her Goth make-up and appearance; Mary was small and plumb. All eyes were trained on Harry Dobbs as he held forth.

'That well-dressed estate agent, that quiet bank clerk, are they law abiding taxpayers?' He stopped and looked around the table. 'Pull away the curtains of your neighbours' house, rip off the roof and look inside. You'll be surprised what you find. Are any of your neighbours' on the sex offender's register?'

'Well I never thought of that,' said Mary clearly startled by the question.

'We run a community action group, helps keep people safe,' Harry asserted eyes blazing. 'We've got something on tonight,' he said looking at Daphne and Mary. Then he glanced at his friend Terry Bishop. 'Why don't you both come along?'

Daphne and Mary paused and looked at each other. The force of Harry Dobbs' personality was hard to resist. Daphne was keener than Mary. Indeed, Daphne was taken with Harry Dobbs.

'Ok,' said Mary. Daphne nodded her head. Harry Dodds produced a piece of paper scribbled his address and gave it to Daphne.

'Here's my address. See you at six o'clock. 'At that he and his friend got up and took his leave.

'What have we got ourselves into!' declared Daphne.

'That is Harry Dobbs. He doesn't work for Talbot's. He works for a company that supplies fruit to us. He's a delivery driver. There's a rumour that he's Robin Hood,' said Mary.

'Robin Hood? He robbed the rich and gave to the poor during the Middle Ages, didn't he?' replied Daphne perplexed.

'That's right. Well, this Robin Hood is a vigilante. He hunts down paedophiles,' said Mary.

'Wow!' exclaimed an astonished Daphne. 'The deadwood stage is rolling on over the plains!'

***

Harry Dobbs lived in an end of terrace house. The narrow pavements were strewn with litter, the street congested with cars. Harry Dobbs answered the door promptly. Mary and Daphne were directed into the front room. The décor was drab, and the room was sparse of pictures and ornaments. There was a central table around which were gathered four chairs. Terry was sitting at the table. On the table was a laptop computer. Harry motioned them to sit down. Harry sat down and stared at the laptop.

'Operation Dandelion is about to start,' declared Harry. Apparently, Harry Dobbs liked flowers, something you would never have guessed from his appearance. 'Now I adopt the persona of a fifteen-year-old girl. I've got ginger hair, I like the colour green, and I like the music of Ariane Grande. I enter a chatroom and call myself Miranda. 'He now concentrated intently on the computer. He had the following exchange in the chatroom.

Miranda: Hi.

David: Hi. Where's your photo?

Miranda: No photo. My mum doesn't like it.

David: How old are you?

Miranda: Fifteen.

David: Same age as me.

Miranda: I love the music of Arianne Grande.

David: So, do I.

Miranda: I'd love to see her in concert.

David: So, would I. What colour is your hair and eyes?

Miranda: I've got ginger hair and green eyes. I'm small and thin.

David: Wow. I'll bet your beautiful.

Miranda: I wish I looked like Ariane Grande. What colour are your eyes?

David: Blue.

Miranda: I like your photo.

David: Why don't we meet up?

Miranda: I'd like that.

David: What about Saturday at two o'clock at the Sanford shopping centre, outside the coffee shop?

Miranda: Sounds great. Can't wait.

David: See you then, love David.

At that point Harry Dobbs logged out of the chatroom; each party trying to deceive the other.

'There, the fish is on the hook,' Harry declared triumphantly to his friend John. He smiled at Daphne and Mary.

'So what happens next?' inquired Daphne.

'The meeting. And we turn the tables on the paedo. 'He looked at Daphne and Mary. 'Society is broken and we're trying to fix it. Come along.'

'Ok,' said Daphne and Mary nodded her head in agreement.

They stayed for a brief drink then took their leave. On the way-out Mary posed a question to Harry Dobbs.

'Why do you call yourself Robin Hood?

'Like Robin Hood I'm on a moral crusade to protect the weak and to fight evildoers,' he declared with certainty.

***

Miranda (aka Harry Dobbs) had agreed to meet her chatroom friend at the local shopping centre. David was meant to be a fifteen-year-old boy, thin build with dark hair and blue eyes. Mary and Daphne met up with Harry Dobbs and Terry near the agreed meeting point.

Harry and Terry seemed energised and pumped up with adrenaline. John paced to and fro. Harry told Terry to stop pacing. Mary and Daphne looked on with apprehension. These situations tended to follow a pattern: confrontation then the humiliation of the target.

'Watch and learn,' said the normally taciturn Terry.

All four kept a look out for a man who appeared to be waiting for someone. People, young and old, came and went. The centre was thronged with people. Mums with prams, giggling teenagers staring at their mobile phones, stern looking security guards. Then out of the milling crowd they spotted a man who could be the target; his eyes were scanning the area as if he were looking for someone. He then stopped outside the coffee shop. He was in his thirties, overweight and casually dressed. This was their man. Harry and Terry glanced at each other and smiled; a smile of triumph. Mary and Daphne glanced at each other knowing that a confrontation was imminent.

Harry and Terry approached the man; Terry produced his smartphone, activating the video on his device. Now Harry was in front of the man, staring directly at him. The man looked nervous.

'You must be David. I'm Miranda!' declared Harry. The man looked stricken. 'You're a paedophile aren't you!'

'I don't know what you're talking about,' the man protested looking around him. He suddenly rushed away, heading for the nearest exit. Shoppers stopped and looked at the commotion; a security guard approached the area but by this time the furore had ended. Harry, Terry, Daphne and Mary decided not to pursue the man.

'Got it all on my phone,' declared Terry.

'What happens now,' inquired Mary.

'Well we upload the video to social media sites. Someone will recognise him. We'll pass the video on to the police. Publicly the police criticise us but off the record their grateful,' said Harry.

'Wow that was an experience,' declared Daphne. She glanced at Mary.

'We'd best be off now,' said Mary to Harry.

'Sure. I'll see you soon,' he replied staring at Daphne. She smiled back at him, her eyes twinkling. Then Mary and Daphne took their leave.

***

Mary had come into a small inheritance after her uncle had passed away. She received a small amount of money and a very unusual object: a crossbow. She invited her friend Daphne to her house to see this remarkable object. Mary lived on a council house estate with her mother. That afternoon her mother was at her dancing class, so Mary was alone when Daphne arrived.

'Hi, come upstairs. I'll show you the crossbow,' said Mary warmly greeting her friend. Amidst the clutter of her bedroom, there was a case on a table. Mary opened the case and there before them was a crossbow.

'Awesome!' declared Daphne looking on in wonder.

'Beautiful isn't it. I'll show you how to use it. 'She lifted it out of the case. At the same time, she took out a bolt from the case. 'Here is the bolt, a small arrow like projectile. Now you pull back the bow and lock it. Then you place the bolt in the groove. Then take aim. 'She lifted the crossbow and took aim. 'Then you depress the lever. 'She showed Daphne the lever. 'That fires the bolt.'

'Move over Buffy the Vampire Slayer!' declared Daphne.

'Too right. You don't mess with the crossbow queen!' said Mary. 'Daphne,' she said her tone becoming more solemn.

'Yes,' said Daphne.

'Do you really like Harry Dobbs?' Mary asked tiptoeing around the subject.

'Yes, I do,' said Daphne.

'Please be careful Daphne,' implored Mary.

***

A pillory was a form of medieval punishment. A wooden frame erected on a vertical post it consisted of three holes, one larger than the other two. The large hole was for the head, the smaller holes for the wrists. A pillory was often found on public crossroads or public places. Crimes such as public intoxication, swearing or perjury were punished by being locked in a pillory. The wrongdoer, locked in the pillory, would be verbally abused by crowds, pelted with objects such as dead animals or excrement. The object of the pillory was to humiliate or shame the wrongdoer.

Harry Dobbs had an acute sense of English history. He once saw an actual pillory in Cheshire. He studied it with intense interest. The pillory excited his imagination. His friend Terry Bishop was a carpenter and joiner. Harry Dobbs decided that he would build a pillory, enlisting the help of his friend. He would build the pillory in Mayflower woods, in a part of the woods not too far from the main road. This would be a secret enterprise; he would not seek the permission of the local authority.

The construction of the pillory required a post to be fixed into the soil; and then a wooden frame to be placed over it in a horizontal position. The wooden frame was divided into two so that the head and hands could be inserted into the appropriate slots. A padlock ensured that the person was securely locked into the wooden frame.

Harry Dobbs had a specific purpose in mind for the pillory.

***

'Help me!'

A woman walking through Mayflower woods thought she heard faint cries for help. She decided to change her usual route and take a short cut through the woods. It was early morning; she was on her way to work. She stopped to listen.

'Help me!'

This time she heard a cry for help. She headed for the trees and bushes, from where the cry for help originated. She came upon a small patch of grassland and was confronted by the most extraordinary spectacle. She could not quite believe her own eyes.

There stood a wooden structure in the shape of a cross. Locked into this wooden structure was a fully grown man. His head protruded from a large hole in the horizontal piece of wood and his hands were locked in two smaller holes.

'Get me out of here!' the man shouted.

'Of course. I'll call the police,' said the woman.

Across the horizontal piece of wood were painted the words I am a paedophile. The police soon arrived and with the aid of a bolt cutter (a padlock was used to lock the man into the horizontal piece of wood) they eventually managed to release the man. The man was then taken to the police station to make a statement.

As the two police officers walked away with distressed young man, they looked at the wooden structure.

'What is that?' asked the bigger of the two.

'That's a pillory,' answered the smaller of the two.

***

Mary and Daphne were joined in Talbot's canteen by their colleague Henry as they sipped their coffee. Henry, a young man in his twenties, had a reputation as a nerd amongst his colleagues. He tended to be verbose and had a vast wealth of obscure information.

'Well ladies see the news?' he inquired.

'No,' said Mary.

'A man was found in Mayflower woods locked in a pillory. On the piece of wood was written I am a paedophile.'

'What's a pillory?' inquired Daphne.

'A pillory is a wooden structure in which a person's head and arms would be locked into a horizontal piece of wood. It was used as a form of punishment in the Middle Ages. Then the person would be pelted with dead animals or excrement!' he said with a flourish.

'Charming,' said Mary.

'And you say the words I am a paedophile were written across the piece of wood?' inquired Mary.

'That's right. The police reported that the victim was a known sex offender,' he confirmed.

'This is the work of vigilantes!' declared Daphne.

'Robin Hood!' declared Mary glancing at Daphne. 'But, is he a good guy?

'Wait a minute. You know who Robin Hood is?' interjected Henry, a puzzled expression on his face.

'Yes,' said Mary. It's Harry Dobbs. 'Henry looked stunned.

'Well we don't know for sure that it was Robin Hood,' said Daphne.

'Last week a man's front door was daubed with the word Paedo Scum. The only thing was the vigilantes' made a mistake,' revealed

Henry.

'Oh yeah. How?' inquired Mary.

'The man was a paediatrician, a doctor who looks after children. The vigilantes' didn't know the difference between a paediatrician and a paedophile!' said Henry.

'Wow!' declared Daphne.

***

The attraction between Daphne and Harry Dobbs was mutual. They had exchanged phone numbers. As far as Daphne was concerned the heart went where the heart went. No explanation was required.

Daphne had received a text from Harry on Monday morning. They were doing a sting operation that night. She was invited to join them at Harry's house. Daphne texted back; she'd be there. This time Mary was not invited.

***

Mary saw a news report on the local news channel. A car had been set on fire. The police were investigating. The owner of the car was a known paedophile. The work of Robin Hood? Mary felt this was the work of Robin Hood. The song about Robin Hood said that he was feared by the bad and loved by the good. Well, this Robin Hood was feared by the good and the bad.

Unusually Mary received a text from Henry. The contents of the text were unbelievable and alarming. The text read: HD. Wolf in sheep's clothing. Has criminal record for sexual assault. Mary's reply to the text read simply: oh my God.

***

The door was opened by Harry Dobbs. Daphne smiled at Harry, and he smiled back. He motioned her to the front room. Daphne noticed that some of the wallpaper on the wall near the ceiling was peeling off. His open laptop was on the table. Terry was sitting at the table drinking a can of beer. He glanced at Daphne as she came in the room. Harry sat in front of his computer and concentrated on the screen.

'Sit down,' he motioned for her to sit down. 'We've got another fish on the hook Daphne. His name is Peter. Claims to be a fifteen-year-old boy. But Peter's no fifteen-year-old,' declared Harry.

'He'll get his comeuppance,' asserted the normally taciturn Terry.

Daphne became suddenly aware of Terry, his massive frame obscuring the chair on which he sat. He happily played Friar Tuck to Harry's Robin Hood. But Friar Tuck had a benign presence. Terry, by contrast, had a silent, menacing presence. His eyes were lifeless. Harry looked up from the computer and smiled at her. She began to feel uncomfortable and regretted her decision to come. She wished Mary was here.

***

Mary knew Daphne was in grave danger. She rushed home. She had phoned Daphne several times: the calls went straight to voicemail. She had texted Daphne several times: no reply.

She picked up the crossbow and two bolts from her bedroom. She placed them in her backpack; they fitted perfectly. Would she use the crossbow? Harry Dobbs was capable of violence; so yes, she would in order to protect her friend. She guessed that Harry Dobbs had an operation this evening. So, he was probably at home on his laptop laying a trap for some unsuspecting paedophile. It was very possible that Daphne was at his house with him. She had a gut feeling.

Harry Dobbs' house was within walking distance. She approached his end of terrace house, trying to find an access point. There was an alleyway at the rear of the house. She decided to scale the wall that separated Harry's house from the alleyway. It wasn't too high; she managed to climb it with relative ease. She jumped from the wall into the garden overgrown with grass and weeds. She approached the house and noticed two windows. She investigated one of the windows and noticed a washing machine. She lifted the window, and it was not locked. Her heart was beating fast now. She had no idea what would confront her once she entered the house.

She climbed into the utility room. She dropped quietly on to the floor of the utility room. She could hear distant voices in another room. She could see a hallway through a crack in the door that faced her. She immediately recognised Daphne's voice.

'I want to go home Harry. 'Her voice was different; it was a pleading, frightened voice.

'You can go home when we've had a bit of fun. But first you've got to take off your T-shirt,' declared a man's voice. This was Harry.

Mary began to tremble. Despite this she took off her backpack and unzipped it. She now had to summon all her courage, like a soldier going into battle. She removed the crossbow. She pulled back the bow and fixed it tight to the appropriate part of the crossbow. She fetched a bolt and placed it in the groove on the crossbow. The bolt was now ready to be launched. She held the crossbow firmly. All this had required her total and absolute concentration.

It was a short hallway. The hallway led to the front door. A door was open on the left side of the hallway. The voices came from the open door. She could hear three voices, Daphne, Harry and Terry.

The moment of truth had arrived. She had to confront Harry and Terry otherwise Daphne was going to be hurt. Once she had stepped inside the house she had stepped inside another world, a world where civilisation had vanished.

She moved swiftly and silently to the open door. Harry and Terry turned abruptly to Mary at the open door. Mary held the crossbow and pointed at Harry. A dark shadow appeared to cross his face; he looked with fierce intensity at Mary.

'Wow look Daphne, it's the seventh cavalry!' said Harry sarcastically.

Terry remained still, staring at Mary; he was clearly ready to unleash violence.

'Daphne come to me,' said Mary, her voice shaking.

Daphne was sitting on a settee sandwiched between Harry and Terry. When she stood up Harry suddenly grabbed her by the neck and got her in a chokehold.

'Don't move Daphne,' Harry said with lethal coldness.

'If you don't let her go I'll shoot you,' Mary asserted, the crossbow still trained on Harry.

Harry stared at Mary with a manic glint in his eyes. Terry remained on the settee. The standoff lasted about two minutes, that to Mary felt like an eternity. Harry held Daphne with his right arm in a chokehold; his left shoulder presented a clear target. Mary took aim at his left shoulder and fired the crossbow. The bolt sank into his left shoulder and Harry let out a cry of pain. Released from the chokehold Daphne ran toward Mary.

Terry suddenly leapt from the settee and surged toward Mary. There was a chair to the immediate right of Mary, and she kicked it in front of her. The upturned chair landed in front of the enormous frame of Terry, and he crashed to the floor like a downed elephant.

Mary and Daphne made a hasty exit from the house. They ran down the street. Mary looked back; no one was pursuing them. Mary phoned the police. Both Harry and Terry were arrested. They were charged with several offences. Their actions as vigilantes revealed their true selves. This Robin Hood was a fraud.

Surreal.

Available worldwide from Amazon

Michael Terence Publishing

www.mtp.agency

www.facebook.com/mtp.agency

@mtp_agency

Printed in Great Britain
by Amazon

26871200R00118